SCANLINES

TODD KEISLING

PERPETUAL
MOTION
MACHINE
PUBLISHING

www.Pe........ing.com

Cover......eysen
Interior Art.....Keisling

Perpetual Motion Machine Publishing
Cibolo, Texas

Scanlines
Copyright © 2020 Todd Keisling

All Rights Reserved

Second Edition 2021

ISBN: 978-1-943720-58-3

www.PerpetualPublishing.com

Cover Art by Matthew Revert
Interior Art by Todd Keisling

ALSO BY TODD KEISLING

AUTHOR'S NOTE

This story contains and deals extensively with graphic depictions of suicide.

Regardless of who you are, where you are, or your circumstances, suicide is never the answer. No matter how alone or hopeless you may feel, someone is always willing to be there and listen.

If you or someone you know is struggling with suicidal thoughts, please do not hesitate to call the Suicide Prevention Hotline: **1-800-273-8255.**

It's free, private, and 24/7. You are heard, you are seen, and you matter. Above all else, **you matter. I** promise.

PLEASE LEAVE THE ROOM IF THIS WILL AFFECT YOU

An Introduction from the Publisher

THE FIRST TIME I saw somebody commit suicide, it was Budd Dwyer. Unlike the kids in *Scanlines*, I did not accidentally stumble across the video while trying to download pornography. Instead, my mother had rented me a movie called *Traces of Death* from Hollywood Video. If you are not familiar with *Traces of Death*, you are already a healthier person than I am, so congratulations.

Released in 1993, *Traces of Death* can be considered a copycat of a far-more successful film titled *Faces of Death* (1978). Both of these films featured clips of gruesome violence presented under a shockumentary narrative. Mondo films, basically— a subgenre of exploitation films designed to look like documentaries, typically depicting atypical, controversial subject matter. Although *Faces of Death* did include clips of real violence and death (of humans *and* animals), the majority of the film is staged. This is where *Traces of Death* differed from its predecessor, because nothing—as far as I can tell—in *Traces of Death* is staged.

Like I said, this was a movie available to rent at *Hollywood Video*, and my mother didn't bat an eye when I picked it up off the shelf. I was eleven years old. I'd heard about *Faces of Death* for years, and had always wanted to see it. When I saw *Traces of Death* available to rent, my brain mistakenly assumed it was the same movie, and I knew this was my only chance. So she rented it for me, and later that night, in my bedroom, I watched it in its entirety.

According to Wikipedia, here are the clips spotlighted in *Traces of Death*:

- The 1993 murder of Maritza Martin Munoz
- The 1988 police chase of armed bank robber Phillip Hutchinson
- The 1980 Iranian Embassy siege
- The 1989 suicide attempt of Terry Rossland
- An animal control officer—Florence Crowell—being attacked by a pitbull in Los Angeles, California in 1987
- The 1984 race car accident of Ricky Rudd
- The 1992 accident of the monster truck Bad Medicine
- The 1967 Caesar Palace jump stunt accident of Evel Knievel
- The 1990 Dinamo–Red Star riot
- The 1992 Maracanã Stadium collapse
- Anatoly Kvochur's plane at the 1989 Paris Air Show crashing after a birdstrike
- The 1987 press conference suicide of R. Budd Dwyer

PLEASE LEAVE THE ROOM IF THIS WILL AFFECT YOU

Most of these I thankfully do not remember now, except for one. The last clip. That Budd Dwyer suicide video. Even now, almost twenty years later, I can still see it play out in my head if I concentrate hard enough. The leadup to the suicide. Seeing a man, broadcasted on live TV—utterly defeated, exhibiting a bizarre calmness as he hands out various packets of documents to people in the room. Then, well, what happens next. Either you already know, or you don't. If you aren't familiar with the Budd Dwyer story, then you'll learn enough about it in Todd Keisling's novella. Although, in *Scanlines*, Todd wisely uses a fictional placeholder named Benjamin Hardy.

Instead of digging deeper into the background of R. Budd Dwyer, and what led to his very public suicide, I'd rather focus on my own reaction to the video. Eleven years old, alone in my room, *Traces of Death* reaching its numbing conclusion. The characters in *Scanlines* are a little older when they see the video. They're seventeen, nearing the end of high school. And even then, they can't comprehend what they've just watched, and neither could I. This was not the first time I'd seen images of an actual dead person. I grew up during the golden age of Rotten Dot Com (kids, do *not* look that up), which I thought had prepared me to withstand even the most hardcore content. But still. There was something about that video. Something about watching an actual *suicide*. To witness a real human being take his life. To hear the bystanders scream. To linger on the man's face, post-gunshot, watching the blood exit his head.

The video changed something in me. Made me start thinking about the universe in a different way.

No matter what people tried telling you, this was in no way a *safe* world. Sometimes people collapsed. Sometimes they broke. If it could happen to them, it could happen to you—which was something I'd really grow to understand a couple years later as a teenager, sitting on the edge of a hotel window, trying to find the "courage" to jump. I never did, and I'm grateful for that, but I'm not ignorant: there is a reality somewhere where I did exactly that—*jump*. There is a reality somewhere where we all succumb to complete internal annihilation, and nothing in this world scares me more. That's what the Budd Dwyer video implanted in my brain. Not an idea, but a realization. One of the most depressing epiphanies an eleven-year-old kid can ever experience.

So imagine my reaction to reading Todd Keisling's *Scanlines*—a novella that felt ripped straight from my own childhood. Even the kids here remind me of myself. They spend their days playing *GoldenEye* on the Nintendo 64 and downloading illegal content on their computers. The narrator's first job is even at Walmart, which was also *my* first job. You might as well be describing myself here, along with countless other children raised in the '90s. And, just like myself, they also stumble upon a politician's suicide video. A video that haunts each and every one of them. It *changes* them. It's a coming-of-age cheat code—one that comes with dire consequences.

Scanlines is many things. It's a bildungsroman, but it's also a ghost story. And, in some ways, a slasher. It reminds me a little bit of *A Nightmare on Elm Street*, too, but saying much more would only further spoil the plot.

PLEASE LEAVE THE ROOM IF THIS WILL AFFECT YOU

If you've made it this far, I hope you continue. *Scanlines* is not an easy read. I assume that much was clear from Matthew Revert's rather gruesome cover art, which practically serves as its own content warning. This book is not going to make you feel good about yourself, or about the world. It is as dark as they come. It is going to unsettle you.

To quote Robert Budd Dwyer, shortly before committing suicide on public television: "Please, please leave the room if this will . . . if this will affect you."

Max Booth III
February 24, 2021

For the friends I had when I was young, and the ones I lost along the way.

▷ PLAY

September 23, 2019

For Robby Goodwin,

He's here again. Inside this time. Covering the windows didn't work. I've been haunted by this dead man's face since I was seventeen, and I can't do it anymore. I can't take that vacant look in his eyes, or the way he seems to be accusing me. Condemning me.

Last month, he took Jordan. Now he's come for me. He's going to take me, and

I'm going to let him because I can't deal with his face anymore. He's death, Robby. Maybe we knew it that night. Maybe . . .

It doesn't matter. It's my turn at the lectern, Robby. I can't carry this torch on anymore. It has to end with us. Should've ended with us back in '98.

I keep thinking about the last time I saw you, the way you dismissed me and told me to leave you alone. I don't blame you, Robby. I want you to know that. Want you to know I didn't give up, that I tried to handle it all on my own. You'll find that proof here in these notes.

I'm sorry. God, I'm so sorry.

■ STOP

I'VE READ DANNY'S suicide note six times, hoping that maybe I can will its truth into lies. It's a joke, a big prank he and Jordan have pulled on me, one that's lasted twenty years and any moment now I expect my phone to ring with both on the other end, laughing and mocking me for falling for it so easily. God, I wish that would happen.

But it won't. My old friends are dead whether I like it or not.

Danny Chambers's little brother, Jordan, took his own life a month ago. My mother called to deliver the news, asked if I would make it home for the funeral. I lied and said I couldn't, had a work deadline I couldn't afford to miss, would send flowers. I didn't do that either. Didn't want Danny to try and track me down. We hadn't spoken since college, and I didn't want that to change.

So how did Danny get my address? I've no idea. Maybe he kept tabs on me after all these years. Maybe the dead man told him where to find me.

I left work early when my mother texted and said Danny was in the news. "Tied a belt around his neck," she said. "Hung himself in his closet."

She gave me the gossip around town. He'd died alone in a one-bedroom apartment on the other side of Moore Hill, soaked in his own urine and a needle sticking out of his arm. Poor bastard. We all found our ways to cope with what happened in '98. Jordan turned to religion and Danny to drugs, and in the end, their vices couldn't save them. I suppose mine won't save me either, but I'm going to write this down anyway.

I'm sitting here in my apartment with a stack of worn and stained notebooks on my coffee table. They were waiting for me when I got here, wrapped up in a brown envelope, my name scribbled in a script I'd recognize anywhere. Danny always had horrible handwriting.

The suicide note rests on top, a final testimony to his tragic life, and I can't decide if I should contact the police or not.

Would it change anything? The coroner confirmed his suicide, chalking him up as another statistic for the area's widespread opiate problem, and he had no next of kin. His folks died in a car crash in the early aughts, right after we finished college, when Danny's habits were just forming. And I'm glad for that, because I don't know if Ron and Debra could handle seeing their oldest son in such a state. Danny's little brother, Jordan, would've been his only kin if Jordan hadn't fallen to his death while hiking at Natural Bridge State Park just last month. The coroner's report concluded Jordan's death was accidental, but I know better. So did Danny.

He's here again.

But did he ever leave? Not by my estimation. I've seen that gray and bloated face every day since that night when we were seventeen. He's here right now, looking through my window. Hi, dead man. I can see you, and I know you can see me. You always have.

I tried to move on with my life after I left home, but the dead man wouldn't let me. He's always with us, attached to our souls like a leech, and sooner or later we knew he would suck us dry. It's funny how one night of adolescent curiosity changed our lives forever. Almost doesn't seem fair, but I guess you could say the same about youth in general. It's all wasted on the young; we just wasted ours a little sooner than everyone else.

Maybe my commentary to Danny's therapy diaries will give some context. Maybe these words will serve as a warning and let the dead man rest.

To whomever finds my confession, heed these words: I've been haunted by a dead man's face since I was seventeen.

Last month, the dead man claimed Jordan Chambers. Two days ago, he claimed Jordan's older brother, Danny.

Tonight, he's come for me.

Outside, the storm is raging, and the pale face of a man dead forty years stares through my apartment window, his eyes rolled up and bulging, his skin bloated and streaked with black trails of coagulated blood. He presses his face against the window when he sees me watching, leaving black smudges on the glass.

I live on the fourth floor of my building.

March 31st, 2016

First entry in a while. Been seeing a therapist, Dr. Marlow, after my last panic episode. Nearly lost my job over that one. Boss let me keep it if I agreed to get help, and here I am, writing shit down again to clear my head. All it's doing is dragging things up from the murk, pulling them out of the shadows. ~~I keep thinking about that night.~~

Doc says the face is a Jungian archetype, whatever that means. Some sort of metaphor created by my mind to help me make sense of past trauma. I keep telling him the truth, but he keeps pushing for more, like he expects I'm going to have some big revelation, some breakthrough that turns me into a fucking case study.

Whatever.

All right, Doc. You win. Let's talk about my trauma. Let's talk about the dead man.

II PAUSE

TO UNDERSTAND THE dead man, you need to understand how we found him. Or how he found us.

Growing up as a computer geek in Stauford, Kentucky during the 90s wasn't fun. "Geek" was a four-letter word in those days and wasn't something to be proud of like it is today. Computers, video games, tabletop gaming, good grades, and the slightest interest in books earned you a merit badge in Geekery which followed you for the rest of your pitiful social life whether you liked it or not. Making friends was something of a luxury when everything you loved was anathema to the rural masses. I guess that's why I bonded so well with those guys back in the day, and why it hurts so much now.

Me and Danny and Jordan were three geeks who happened to bond over arcade games back in elementary school, and the friendship sort of stuck. I mean, who else would want to be your friend because you got the high score in *Mortal Kombat* at Rose's Department Store downtown? We each shared a passion for all things electronic, from gadgets to video games to computers, and it wasn't long before we were hanging out together on the weekends.

Danny and Jordan's house became the Mecca of our weekend pilgrimages, partly because they had a Nintendo 64 and partly because they had the best dial-up connection in the area. For Jordan's birthday one year, their parents had a second phone line installed just so the internet connection wouldn't be interrupted. They were constantly playing online games, chatting with friends on ICQ, or downloading music.

I'm talking about pre-Napster here, when you had to go to chatrooms using a relay client and request individual songs, sit in a queue, and hope your connection didn't time out before the download finished. Completely anonymous and no tracking. You sign on, join your chat of choice, and submit a request for your file. Ten minutes to an hour later, you'd have a copy of whatever you wanted, from music to games to movies. All free. All illegal, but we didn't think about things like that. It was a simpler time.

Most weekends, we spent hours in front of the TV down in the den, usually playing game after game of *GoldenEye* on the Nintendo 64 while The Smashing Pumpkins or Nirvana blared from their computer's tinny speakers. We'd eat pizza for dinner and talk about school or girls, sometimes both. We told stupid jokes usually involving farts or dicks or someone's mother.

There was no bedtime and no one to scold us for cursing, no one to tell us to stop being teenagers for five minutes and mind our manners. No judgment and no boundaries. No one to make fun of us for being geeks, no one threatening to kick our asses for being different.

Considering the stark contrast of our living situations, I'm surprised I wasn't at their house more often in those days. I lived with my mom in a rented trailer on the far side of town, and we didn't have a phone because Mom couldn't afford one. My parents split when I was a baby, and I only saw my dad once a month. What few video games I owned came from my old man on Christmas and my birthday. Mom worked two jobs and could barely afford rent, and while she did the best she could, I inherited some of that stress. No kid should have to worry about the bills being paid.

When I was sixteen, I got a job pushing shopping carts at the local Walmart and used my meager wages to pay for my own internet access. My dad gifted me his old Ford Tempo and helped pay the premium on my insurance for the first year, completing a vicious cycle of working to afford a car so I could drive to work. I found myself in a position not unlike my mother, working just to scrape by, and scraping by just to work.

I'd like to think Danny and Jordan's folks knew the sort of home I came from. I'd like to think they were trying to offer an environment that wasn't stifled by the discomfort of poverty. They welcomed me into their home with open arms, didn't judge me for where I came from. I look back on those days fondly. I wish it all hadn't ended after that night.

I remember the night clearly—a Friday night bleeding into Saturday morning, a storm raging overhead just like tonight. Ron and Debra Chambers were upstairs in bed and might as well have been on the moon. Scott Weiland sang "Pretty Penny" while the menu for *GoldenEye* lit up the family room. Me, Danny, and Jordan were huddled around the family computer, crawling porn sites in search of Jenna Jameson. I don't remember whose idea it was to log in to mIRC and download one of her movies—probably Jordan's, though it easily could've been any one of us— and after venturing upstairs to make sure the coast was clear, Danny queued up a video for download.

It's funny how certain things remain stuck in your memory, little inconsequential details like errant grains of sand between your toes, gritty things you can't quite shake out. I don't remember what we were wearing or what song played after Stone Temple Pilots. I remember every second of watching the download progress bar inch forward, the three of us held in eternal suspense at the mercy of a 56k dial-up connection. And I remember the camaraderie, a weird sort of bonding between three friends over seeing a big-breasted woman suck another man's dick. Hormones are weird, and so are teenagers.

"I'm serious," Jordan said, when the download hit 50% completion. "Her tits are out to here. Fuckin' huge. Like two giant cantaloupes."

He cupped the air in demonstration. I remember laughing and telling him he wouldn't know what to do with them; I remember the way he blushed with embarrassment, the way his reddened face looked purple in the gloom. We might've played *GoldenEye* for a while to kill time, but my memory is hazy. I remember Danny's excitement when the download bar reached 99% two hours later. We were nearly delirious at that point, struggling to stay awake and punch drunk, laughing at our own stupidity.

"Guys," Danny said, swiveling in the computer chair. He lowered his voice and beamed. "It's done."

We huddled around the CRT monitor and watched in anticipation as Danny closed all the windows on screen and double-clicked the video file. We were seventeen going on stupid, our better judgment tossed aside in the name of adolescent horniness, and I don't think any of us even bothered to read the file name.

The video was not what we thought it would be.

A grainy monochrome palette lit up the den, highlighting the scanlines on the monitor, and fizzy audio leaked from the speakers like spilled soda. A crowd of people were gathered in a room with white walls, seated sporadically in rows of wooden chairs all pointed toward an empty lectern in the center of the frame. An American flag stood in one corner, the stars and stripes distorted by wrinkled fabric.

"What the hell is this?"

Danny's voice punctuated the gloom and stood out in contrast to the fizz and pop of the audio, but we didn't dare tear our eyes away from the screen.

"Maybe it's retro porn," Jordan said, breathless.

None of us moved, waiting impatiently for something to happen, dreading what might happen without the slightest clue what would. Murmurs from the crowd of men and women on screen dulled as a large man in a three-piece suit entered the room. He approached the lectern with a folder in one hand, a paper bag in the other.

I turned to Danny, ready to beg him to turn off the video, but the man in the suit began to speak. His words were distorted, choppy, the audio cutting in and out and at times muted as if submerged underwater. But we still understood what he was saying. For as long as I live, I will never forget.

The man in the suit spoke for a few minutes, and just as some of the people in his audience were about to leave, he pulled something from the paper bag. He told them all to sit down, told them to stay back. Someone might get hurt.

Even at a distance, the silver revolver looked huge in the grainy man's hand. Jordan gasped when he realized what was happening, and Danny scrambled for the mouse to minimize the screen, but computers in those days weren't as reliable. Windows 98, you know, it locked up and didn't respond sometimes, and did so at that moment.

Me, I wanted to look away, but I couldn't bring myself to do so. Knowing what was happening, I was drawn to the mystery of uncharted waters. I'd never seen someone die before, much less willingly take their own life, and the appeal of witnessing something for the first time overpowered the utter horror I felt in my gut. We'd forgotten about the promise of Jenna Jameson's naked breasts, our arousal displaced by something far more primal—the need to feel alive, a feeling of "at least that's not me," the promise of death renewing the purpose of life. I wanted to look away, but if given a moment to go back and change things, I think I'd still watch.

In the end, we witnessed this man's heinous demise. He shoved the gun barrel against the roof of his mouth, pulled the trigger, and pop goes the weasel. A flowery pattern of blood and brains sprayed the wall behind him. The force of the gunshot propelled him backward against the wall where he collapsed in a heap, his head rolling forward chin to chest, a thick stream of blood oozing from his nostrils and mouth.

We watched in horrified silence, unable to move or speak or breathe. The camera slowly zoomed in on the dead man's face, on his empty eyes staring accusingly at us as if we were to blame for his predicament. We didn't know him then, didn't know who he was, didn't know why he'd done what he'd done. And it didn't matter. We were watching him die, over and over again. The video played on a loop four more times before Jordan took over the mouse and closed the window.

I stared at the desktop. The video file was still highlighted: NICE_SHOT_DUNCAN.avi.

"I'm going to be sick."

Danny shot up from the chair and raced into the bathroom. We heard him heaving for the next ten minutes. Jordan sat at the desk, slowly rocking back and forth, shaking his head in disbelief. As for me, I felt the same nausea as Danny, but there was also an emptiness I couldn't place, a sudden cavern inside me like the whole world had dropped away. The outline of the dead man's face was burned into my retinas, and whenever I closed my eyes, I saw him in squiggly lines and flashing colors. He was still bleeding, still staring, still dead.

I don't think any of us really slept that night. Or any night since.

■ S T O P

April 24th, 2016

Saw the dead man's face on one of my coworkers and lost my shit. Working on an assembly line with machines that can tear off a finger or arm if you're not careful isn't the time or place to lose your shit. Eugene wore the face, and he didn't understand when I screamed and backed away from him. I tripped over a crate and fell backward, hit my head on the adjacent conveyor belt. Walsh had to hit the emergency stop on the line so nothing would pile up, and before I knew it, all the managers were down from their office and standing over me, snapping their fingers and asking me if I was okay, did I hit my head, was I going to file a workman's comp claim.

I took the day off. Stopped on the way and bought a dime from Kenny. Smoked half of it before this.

I can't get it out of my head, you know. The dead man was on Eugene's face. Covering his face, like a mask. For a split instant I saw the dead man walking toward me, dripping blood, his eyes rolled up in his head. His head glitched with fuzzy static and scanlines like bad VHS tracking.

The meds ain't working.

Nothing's working. ~~I think about ending it all but I'm afraid it won't stop even if I do.~~ The dead man is only haunting me here. What will he do to me when I'm dead?

‖ PAUSE

I WAS UP EARLY, already dressed when Ron and Debra came downstairs to make breakfast, and I joined them like I did every weekend. Danny and Jordan stumbled in not long after, and we avoided looking at one another. Debra asked her sons if they slept well, and neither of them said anything. They didn't have to. The circles under their eyes said enough.

What we'd witnessed changed us in ways none of us understood. We were unwittingly burdened with emotions we weren't equipped to express. Not at seventeen. Maybe not ever.

In the days that followed, I struggled to fall asleep, and when I did, I was haunted with nightmares of the video. I'd find myself in the audience of the press conference, crying out to stop the guy from taking his life, and when I'd look around to beg the others to stop him, I'd find they were plastic mannequins in wigs, their faces missing and heads hollow. When I'd try to climb out of my seat, I'd discover I was also made of plastic, my pallid arms cracked and splintered, the paint chipping away. The dead man always looked at me as he put the gun in his mouth, and when he pulled the trigger, a waterfall of thick black slime spilled from his nostrils.

I always woke up with the taste of metal in my mouth, the acrid odor of gunpowder in my nostrils. Toward the end of that first week, I was sneaking shots of my mom's bottle of peach schnapps she kept in the cabinet above our refrigerator. The alcohol weighed me down and took me deeper into my head when I slept. The dreams weren't as bad then. To this day, I can't sleep without a nightcap of schnapps. It's disgusting.

Danny and Jordan and I kept our distance from one another for a few days after. In happier times, we were always together, talking about the latest games or music or some stupid website Jordan had found, but after the weekend, everything else seemed so insignificant, temporary. Seeing one another was a reminder of the horrible moment we'd shared, and I think we were all afraid to talk about it for fear it might conjure memories of the man's suicide.

Not that I could help it. I can't speak for my friends, but while I was struggling to get the dead man's bleeding face out of my mind, I also discovered I couldn't stop thinking about him. Who was he? Why did he do what he did? And what sick fuck would send that video out into the world?

Toward the end of the week, I spotted Danny sitting by himself in the cafeteria and nursing a bottle of juice. I sat across from him, took in the sallow features of his pale face. The dark circles were embedded below his eyes, purple halos of sleepless nights and restless dreams and memories of a man blowing his brains out over and over again.

"Hey," I said.

"Hey."

"You've been avoiding me."

Danny looked up from his lunch tray and stared at me. "No, I just needed to be alone. Needed to think."

Jordan approached from the lunch line, took a seat beside me. "He's been like this for days. We're having trouble sleeping." He leaned closer, lowered his voice. "I keep seeing him. When I sleep."

I nodded. "Me too. I can't stop thinking about it, and it's fucking me up, guys." I told them about my mom's bottle of peach schnapps and even managed to pry a laugh from them.

"I'm seeing him," Danny began. He paused, measuring his words, twirling his fork in place on the plastic tray. "But not just in my dreams. I saw him yesterday morning behind our house."

Jordan nearly choked on his drink. "And you didn't say anything? What the fuck, D?"

"What the hell could I say, Jordan? Would it have changed anything? It's not like we could make Dad chase him off with a shotgun. Besides, I didn't want to scare Mom."

"Guys," I said. "Come on, stop. Danny, what do you mean you saw him?"

I remember his hands trembled when he spoke, and that's how I knew he believed what he was seeing. Danny wasn't one to show much emotion in those days—he was pragmatic, a thinker, top of his class, a quiet genius destined for medical school. He never stressed and he never got upset. When he told us about what he'd witnessed from the bathroom window, his eyes brimmed with tears, and his hands wouldn't stop shaking.

"It was our neighbor, Mr. Drummond, but it wasn't. He was messed up somehow, like . . . like he was in an old movie. His body was filled with static and wavy lines, his clothes were black and white, and his skin was super pale, and when he turned around, I saw the man from the video. Right after he shot himself. The whole lower half of his face was black with blood. God, he fucking looked right at me, and then he turned around and went back into Mr. Drummond's house." Danny took a deep breath and exhaled slowly. He wiped his eyes. "The whole back half of his head was missing."

Jordan looked at me, and then down at his lunch tray. We gave the table some air and let Danny's words sink in.

"D," Jordan said, "we didn't get a whole lot of sleep, man. I'm tired. You're tired. We're seeing shit, okay?"

I nodded. "Jordan's got a point. I believe you think you saw something, Danny, but let's be real here. The video was a sick joke, a fucked-up prank by some jerk on the internet."

I wanted so badly to believe my own words. I think we all did, but what remained unspoken between us was the gravity of what we'd witnessed. There was something to the video that we couldn't grasp, only felt deep down in our bellies and in our hearts, the way a chill can reach your bones and never leave.

"I want to find out where it came from," Danny said. "I want to know why."

He didn't give us a chance to reply, collected his things and left us sitting in silence. I stared at Jordan and shrugged. "You didn't see anything, did you?"

"No way. Just in my dreams. So fucked up."

Understatement, I thought, replaying the conversation in my head. I'd never seen Danny so upset before. As unsettling as it was, I found relief in knowing we shared the same curiosities. Danny wanted to get to the heart of the matter just as I did.

We were ghouls in a graveyard, digging up a dead man's grave for closure. We never considered he might want to stay buried.

■ S T O P

May 9th, 2016

Thought of our old friend Nelle today. Saw a commercial on TV for The Wizard of Oz, and I thought back to when we directed a play for the elementary school kids to satisfy some National Honor Society obligations. Community service hours. All that fun high school bullshit. We made a good team that year and put on a hell of a show. She made a great Scarecrow.

Christ, I haven't thought of her in years. Never got to say goodbye to her, and part of me never forgave

Robby for getting Nelle involved. I wish I had. Doesn't matter. It happened. Wish it hadn't, but I can't change that now. Robby's washed his hands of me, and maybe Jordan, too.

Last I spoke to J, he didn't seem happy to hear from me, and I guess that's just as well. He'd not heard from Robby in over a year. Glad J is doing well. Seems to be. Little bugger found Jesus, which is fine, I guess. Never took him for a religious man. At least he has peace, or so he says. I'll choose to believe him, even if my heart says otherwise.

But I digress.

Back to the wonderful land of Oz. We watched this film maybe ten times while we were rehearsing our play so we could imitate their backdrops. Reminds me of the old urban legend about this movie. Supposedly, one of the crew fell behind a backdrop and accidentally hung himself. Supposedly, you can see his silhouette hanging from one of the trees in the Tin Man's woods.

The internet tells me it's a hoax, but I'm not so sure. I can see him hanging there right now, like he fell from a black-and-white Kansas, grainy and distorted and leaking black oil from his mouth. When Dorothy and the Scarecrow skip along the Yellow Brick Road, their faces glitch and melt, the whites of their eyes running like eggs, and they turn to stare at me.

The Wizard of Oz is on TV right now. My TV is still unplugged.

Dorothy, Toto, Tin Man, Scarecrow, and the Dead Man all hold hands as their faces gush black ropes of blood.

We're off to the see the Wizard, and I can't stop crying.

‖ PAUSE

DANNY WAS RIGHT to blame me. I did get Nelle involved, and if I'd known then what I know now . . . well, you know how that goes. In my defense, I only did it to help him—to help all of us—thinking that if we could track down the dead man's identity, we might be able to put everything to rest. That's how it works in the movies, right? Find the dead man's bones and give them a proper burial?

Not likely. You can't bury what's already buried; you can only dig it up. We were so stupid to think there would be no repercussions. The whole incident just felt *wrong,* you know? Sort of like the stillness before a storm. You can see the clouds brewing and feel the wind blowing, but you've no clue how bad that rain and lightning will be. Not until it's crashing over your head.

The way Nelle Simmons got involved was because of her affinity for everything audio and video. She was a closet nerd who had friends on both sides of the social aisle. A cross between Janis Joplin and Ani DiFranco, Nelle would've fit in at the height of the counterculture movement in the 60s or the punk scene of the late 70s. Maybe both, simultaneously. That was Nelle's charm, I guess—she was weird and rebellious and didn't give a shit about fitting in. And I had a huge crush on her. So did Danny, although he never admitted it to me. He didn't have to.

Nelle's involvement with the school's A/V club was legendary. She gave up a prominent position in the school's dance team, a decision which earned her the ire of the coach, Mrs. Smith. Coach Smith demanded she choose another extracurricular activity to take its place, expecting Nelle would reconsider her decision; instead, Nelle joined the A/V club and gave Coach Smith the finger. She spent a month in detention for that gesture, but she told me she never regretted it and would never look back. Like I said: weird and rebellious.

As it turned out, Nelle developed a genuine interest in electronics and A/V, and by the time we were seniors, she was considering film school for undergrad. Sometimes I think about what might've been, if she'd had a chance to develop her talents further, but such thoughts usually lead to darker places I'd rather not visit.

So, that's Nelle Simmons in a nutshell. We were paired up for a group project in Chemistry class, an arrangement I engineered for selfish reasons, and asked her about tracing the origins of a video file.

"What do you mean by 'trace?' Like, hunt down where it came from?"

"Yeah," I whispered, keeping an eye on our teacher, Mr. Hart. "You know, like how an image file has data embedded with the date, location, etc.?"

She chewed her lip, thinking. "Well, yeah, like a video file would have similar data. The date it was encoded, the codec used—anyway, what's this about?"

I didn't want to tell her, was already prepared to shut my mouth and tell her it's not important, but she gave me that look. You know the one. Anyone who's ever had a crush on anyone knows what look I'm talking about. It's a look in the eye, a glance of dominance that makes you melt on the inside, turns your stony resolve to butter. It's the power we give the other person, the sort of power that will make us bend to their will at the slightest indication. A power they don't even know they wield. I didn't stand a chance.

"I—that is, me and Danny and Jordan—downloaded a video over the weekend. It's really messed up, and it's . . . well, you'd have to see it to understand."

"Is this like one of those beheading videos from Rotten.com?"

God, there's a website I haven't thought of in years. In the early days of the internet, back in the late 90s, Rotten was a site that lived up to its name: autopsy and crime scene photos, videos of torture and executions, and other bizarre shit. Jordan once found JFK's autopsy photos there, with close-ups of the wound where his brain should've been. Not safe for life or your lunch.

"No, this is something worse."

Her eyes lit up at the sound of mischief and mystery. "So ominous. Fine, I'll meet you after school. We can talk about it then."

She followed me to Danny's house that afternoon. I didn't have a chance to tell him ahead of time, so Nelle's appearance came as a surprise. He pulled me aside and asked me what the hell I was thinking, but our conversation didn't go much farther than that. Nelle interrupted him, asked where his computer was, and trotted along when he pointed her toward the den.

In hindsight, I should've known better than to show up at his house with Nelle Simmons, of all people, especially without giving him a heads up. I wish I could say it didn't come between us, but we were at the height of our social immaturity, and hormones have no loyalty.

I followed Danny down into the den. Jordan sat in front of the TV, playing a game while Nelle watched. She eyed the spare controller but didn't ask to play.

"Nelle," Danny said, "I'm not sure what Robby told you, but I really don't think you should watch this video."

She turned and glared at him. "Are you being sexist?"

Danny's cheeks blossomed red. "What? No, not at all, I just—"

"The video's different," Jordan said, still staring at the TV. He paused the game and looked up at her with swollen eyes. "It messes with your head."

"Whatever," Nelle said. "Just show me so I can get on with my life."

Jordan looked at Danny, who turned to me. *Up to you,* those looks said, and in the end, it was Nelle who sat down at the computer of her own accord. Even if we'd pleaded with her, I think she would've insisted on seeing the video anyway. Nothing we could say would've stopped her. I keep telling myself that, but I can't make my heart believe it.

The screen flickered to life, revealing a desktop crowded with icons. She swirled the mouse pointer around and looked up at Danny. "So, where's this movie you want to show me?"

■ STOP

▷ PLAY

June 12th, 2016

Saw an article on one of those viral news sites today about a face everyone dreams about. Some psychiatrist noticed a pattern with some of his patients. They all described dreams featuring a man with a unibrow, wearing a suit and tie. He always interrupted their dream to give them advice. Marital advice, financial advice, sex advice, whatever— the dream man had something to say about it. The nameless psychiatrist contacted several peers, who all reported something similar. They contacted their peers, and so on. All told, there were thousands of people worldwide who'd dreamed of this "Dream Advisor." Same guy, same face, same unibrow. What could it mean?

Not a goddamn thing. None of it is true. The article was a hoax, a weird social experiment run by a marketing firm to test the gullible nature of the average internet user. Count me among them. No shit.

Whole thing reminded me of what happened after we let Nelle watch the video. God, what a shit-show. Makes me sick to think about it. It wasn't just our mistake anymore.

I started seeing the dead man everywhere. Neighbors. Friends. Mom and Dad. They wore his face like a mask. Scratchy, glitchy, shivering with bad tracking and static. Sometimes I'd wake up at night, catch a glimpse of his figure in my room, slumped in a corner and staring at me with bulging eyes.

And when I dreamed, I'm in his place at that lectern. I'm the one holding the paper bag, and I'm watching all those faceless people in the audience. Listening to them whisper under their breath, listening to them mock me. Watching them roll their eyes at me as I mumble on forever. I keep talking because I know what happens when I stop. I try to keep talking, but I can't. I always reach for the bag—

I've got claw marks on my throat from where I scratch myself in my sleep. I wake up gasping for air and a taste of gunpowder in my mouth. I wake up with the dead man's face in my head.

After the video got out, everyone

began dreaming of the dead man's face. He only had one piece of advice for them.

They were the first to go. He saved the three of us for last.

‖ P A U S E

NELLE'S REACTION TO the video was about what you'd expect. She spent twenty minutes heaving into the toilet, and when she emerged, she told us she couldn't help us and abruptly left. I wish I could say her interest ended there, but the next day at school, she joined us at our corner of the lunch room.

"Would you send me the video tonight?"

I thought Jordan was going to choke on his drink. He looked at Danny, then to me. "Over dial-up? You know how long that'll take?"

Nelle rolled her eyes. "Yes, dipshit. If you guys want me to figure out where the video came from, I'll need to look at the file on my machine."

"You're not going to watch it again, are you?" Danny's concern lit up his face for the first time in days. "I just . . . look, I don't think it's safe, okay?"

An uneasy silence fell between us, and I spoke up to break the quiet. "I'm with Danny. Don't watch it again." Jordan nodded in agreement. Nelle smiled, gathered her backpack and stood from the table.

"Trust me, I have no desire to watch it again. Just send it over ICQ tonight."

We didn't hear from her for three days. After the transfer completed, she signed off from ICQ. She didn't respond to email, and she was absent from school. None of us were forward-thinking or brave enough to ask for her phone number. So, we waited and hoped nothing terrible had happened to her. Danny and Jordan never said so, but I think we were all worried something might.

Nelle returned to school on Friday. She looked haggard, strung out, with bloodshot eyes. Everyone suspected she had the flu, but we knew better. We didn't look much different. She sat with us at lunch and revealed the reason for her absence.

"I know who he is. Was."

We traded glances, stunned by Nelle's admission. Danny crossed his arms. "How?"

"There's a date stamp in the corner of the video. It's hard to see because of all the static and tracking noise. You guys probably didn't even notice." She looked over her shoulder, waited for a group of students to pass by before continuing. "Couldn't sleep, so I spent some time searching online."

Bear in mind this was before Google. Searching for anything online was a chore, especially when all she had to go on was a date and a suicide. I admit I was skeptical until she produced a folder of printed articles. She put the folder on the table and opened it, revealing a grainy black-and-white photo of the dead man haunting us. He looked happy in the photo, smiling proudly at someone off-camera. A round button was affixed to his chest: VOTE HARDY!

Finally, our dead man had a name.

Here are the facts: Congressman Benjamin Hardy

III of Pennsylvania's 6th district. Democrat. Husband of Betsy Lou Hardy and father of John, Winston, and Benjamin Hardy IV. Born and raised in Reading, Pennsylvania. Elected to Congress in 1970. Accused of taking bribes related to a revitalization project concerning his hometown's railways. On the morning of June 3rd, 1987, Hardy called a press conference for which most expected a resignation from his post.

Instead, Hardy asserted his innocence, ranted against the moral and ethical corruption of his Republican opponents, and sent his love to his wife and three boys. When he finished, Congressman Hardy pulled a .357 Magnum from a paper bag, pushed the barrel into his mouth, and blew his brains out. The press conference was broadcast live statewide, as the scandal was top news at the time, interrupting scheduled programming on all local networks. Schools were adjourned for the summer and children were in their homes watching morning cartoons when this seemingly innocent, seemingly boring press conference interrupted their routines and infected their households.

I'd like to think those kids had the sense to turn away and go play outside, but as a child of the 80s, I know better. They waited for the broadcast to end. They watched. Ten years later, so did we.

"Oh my God." Jordan leaned back in his seat, shaking his head in disbelief. "A fucking congressman?"

"They televised it," Danny mumbled. "That's so messed up."

Nelle rubbed her puffy eyes and yawned. "Yeah, tell me about it. I've been fucking dreaming about him. My sleep is all screwed up, and I've felt like shit ever since I watched it with you guys."

Dreams about the dead man weren't anything new to us, and we took turns relaying our experiences to her. She listened, and when we were finished, she told us what we already suspected: her dream was the same as ours, sitting among the audience of terrified onlookers while Hardy ate a bullet.

"This doesn't make sense," Jordan said. "How can we all be dreaming the same thing?"

Nelle's yawn prompted me to do the same. I hadn't been sleeping all that well either, and it was beginning to catch up to me. "Maybe it's trauma," I said, knowing it was a weak suggestion and feeling foolish for even saying it. Danny shook his head.

"It's more than that. I'm seeing him in other places. I saw him this morning in the breakfast line. One of the cafeteria ladies was wearing his face."

Nelle giggled, a pebble which began an avalanche of laughter that lasted the better part of five minutes. The levity was welcome. We were all tired, confused, and unsure of what to do. What *could* we do? We were being haunted by the face of a dead congressman, forced to watch him kill himself over and over in our dreams. Knowing who he was didn't change anything, and over the next several weeks, things grew considerably worse.

▶ FAST FWD

Jordan saw Hardy's bloated and bleeding face on his father that weekend. Ron Chambers was in their garage, changing the oil in his car, and asked Jordan for a wrench. Jordan obliged, knelt beside the car, and saw the dead man's face grimacing back at him.

"Scared the fucking shit out of me, Rob. He was there and not there, like a bad dream you're still seeing even after you wake up. He was bleeding and this awful noise was gurgling from his throat. So much blood."

I watched him shiver. We were outside the school the following Monday, sitting in the sun and waiting for Danny to emerge.

"Does your brother know?"

Jordan shook his head. "Not sure how to tell him. God, I can't get it out of my head. I'm scared of looking at Dad. And I—what the fuck does it mean, man? Why is this happening to us?"

I didn't have an answer for him. My mother played host to Hardy's bloody maw that morning. She'd stuck her head into my room while I was getting dressed to announce breakfast was ready, and when I turned around, I nearly pissed myself. There was Hardy, gray and bleeding and full of static, standing less than five feet away. I stared, swallowed back the taste of bile, and said okay, I'd be there in a minute. Hardy nodded and spoke with mom's voice, said "Hurry up. I'm late as it is."

I thought about telling Jordan but decided not to. He was scared enough, and I didn't want to add to the anxiety. What I had to share with them was worse.

We hadn't spoken since Nelle's revelations earlier in the week, and I'd stayed home that weekend to work on an essay for English class. "Work" was a loose term—I spent most of the time searching the internet for more information on Benjamin Hardy. There wasn't much I could find that Nelle hadn't already provided. Aside from an entry on a government website listing his tenure in office and an obituary from the *Reading Eagle*, Congressman Hardy had vanished from public consciousness.

Tired and frustrated, I stretched out on my bed and stared at the ceiling, struggling to put the pieces together in my head. Someone must've copied the broadcast to VHS cassette, probably sold it to the highest bidder. And who would buy it? I imagined some scrawny, pale thing living in a small apartment, with stacks of VHS cassettes lining the walls. A collection of the unspeakable and disturbed, the worst of pornography, snuff films, rare outtakes from films once thought lost to time.

Did this ghoul even watch the video, or was it another trophy for their collection? Part of me hoped they were being haunted just as we were—

Shit. I'd pointed Nelle in the wrong direction.

Feeling stupid, I returned to my computer and dialed in to the local network. Once connected, I searched for TV stations local to the Reading area, one that would've been present at Hardy's press conference. There were two in the area—WFMZ out of Allentown and WTVE in Reading—and both were present when Hardy pulled the trigger. Then came the hard part: finding the next bread crumb. I knew which stations were there, but I didn't know who was on their camera crews—and that's assuming the person who leaked the tape was even on location that day.

My surge of excitement withered and died. Frustrated, I picked up the copy of *Beowulf* I was supposed to be analyzing and returned to bed. I lay there for a while, skimming pages of Old English poetry and re-reading them because my mind had wandered back to that grainy conference room. Words blended into one another on the page, and sleep found me with my guard down. I'd tried to limit sleep as much as possible, a feat which grew more difficult with each day, and the Anglo-Saxon poetry was my death knell. I sank into an abyss of shadows and smoke, and he was waiting for me there.

Here's what I remember:

I'm standing in a hallway with checkered tile. The air is hazy and smells of smoke, and when I look down at my hands, I'm holding a portfolio of documents and a paper bag. I walk forward, my footsteps echoing in the emptiness, and I hang a right into a conference room I've seen so many times before. There's a lectern on display before rows of wooden chairs occupied with clothed mannequins. Pale faces stare ahead without expression or judgment. Joining them is a large old-time camera set up in the back of the room. I'm talking about something from the turn of the century, impossibly huge with dual film canisters and crank-driven, the sort of thing used in the silent era. Its presence is what unnerves me most, as it's the one thing which seems out of place. It's the totem anchoring me to the knowledge of my dreaming, but unlike other lucid dreams, I am not in control. My actions aren't my own; I'm made to feel as though they are, but at the lift of every step and twitch of every muscle, there is the sensation of something pushing, pulling. I am being guided to the lectern, and soon I will be told what to say. I place the folder on the lectern and open it to the first page which is all scribbles and errant lines, but in my head, I know it says CONFESS AND BE FORGIVEN. My mouth opens and I speak in a voice which is not my own, a shrill and rambling voice like the sound of an abattoir at peak capacity, swine lined up awaiting their execution. I can't understand the words spilling from my mouth, and I look to the pages before me for guidance, but they are nothing more than scribbles and doodles of grinning faces with Xs over their eyes. As my babbling increases, I look to the taciturn audience and discover they've been replaced with my friends: Jordan, Danny, and Nelle sit in silence, solemn expressions pointed forward, seeing and not seeing me. There is another figure now, standing behind the camera and cranking away to record my final moments of insanity, and I already know who he is before he stands tall to reveal his face. Benjamin Hardy glares at me with dead and bleeding eyes, the wound in the roof of his mouth unspooling ropes of coagulated blood, and as he steps away from the camera, I hear the squelching of rotten tissue as it buckles under weight and gravity. I smell gunpowder and death, and I make one last attempt at breaking free of this place, but my body will not cooperate. I'm frozen at the lectern, watching the dead man approach and surrounded by my friends who are now wearing his bleeding face as their own, and there is only one way out. Trembling, I remove the weapon from the paper bag, heave its weight in my hand, and watch as my audience grins victorious. "Stay back," I hear myself say. "Someone might get hurt." And then I shove the barrel against the roof of my mouth, pull the trigger, and witness a white-hot flash of light surge through my retinas as a bullet tears through my brain. White light dissolves into static and noise and scratchy tracking patterns before all goes black, the world around me brought to a full stop.

I've suffered through this dream every night since I was seventeen. Sometimes the people in the audience change, and sometimes the message on the page reads differently—SOONER OR LATER, it once read. WITNESS MY DESPAIR, another time—but Hardy is always there behind the camera, and it always ends with me eating a bullet.

I awoke from that dream in a fit of terror, drenched with panic sweat, the taste of smoke in my mouth. Sunlight filtered through my curtains, washing the room in a warm orange gold, but I felt so cold and spent an hour huddled in my blankets, shivering. Were my friends experiencing the same dream? Were we all going to dream of killing ourselves?

And that's when the idea struck. I returned to my computer, reconnected the modem once more, and conducted a search of suicides in 1987 related to the stations present at Hardy's conference. The search took a couple of hours—there were a lot of obituaries reported by those news stations that year—but then I happened upon an article paying tribute to one of WTVE's cameramen, Clarence Duncan. A corollary search revealed Mr. Duncan was found in his home, dead from a self-inflicted gunshot wound.

The circumstances were too perfect, too coincidental to be unrelated. On a whim, I searched for Duncan's name in relation to Hardy's suicide and discovered a rabbit hole of VHS message board speculation and theories, one feeding into the other. At the end of a lengthy digital tunnel which took me until nightfall to reach, I found three words which pointed us in the right direction: The Duncan Tape.

▶ PLAY

Brandon Helmford's involvement was a point of contention for all of us. He ran with a different crowd, and while Jordan had a couple of classes with him, the three of us didn't have much in common except music. Brandon was a musician and a rich goth kid, with shaggy hair dyed midnight black and a piercing in his left eyebrow. He was active in a few local bands and had even played with the high school band for a semester until he was kicked out for selling pot to a couple of freshmen. Word around school was that he practiced Satanic rituals on the weekends, sacrificing small animals to the Goat Lord—someone's neighbor's brother confirmed it, didn't you know?— but we saw through the bullshit façade. He just wanted a way to stand out from the crowd. Didn't we all?

His mystique aside, Brandon also had connections: his uncle, Thomas, owned a video rental shop in Breyersburg, the next town over. Video Fantastique, it was called. Thomas Helmford was known in the area as being an odd guy, with a massive collection of films in his possession. If anyone knew anything about the Duncan Tape, it would be Thomas Helmford—and to approach him, we needed his nephew Brandon.

Nelle also had a thing for him, which only made me dislike him even more. Same goes for Danny, but he masked his discontent with an equally measured displeasure that Nelle had already told Brandon about the video.

I still remember that phone call, with Danny on one phone in the kitchen while Jordan and I listened from another down in the den.

"Look, I don't want anyone else seeing this thing, okay? You know what effect it has. You said it yourself, you're having the dreams and seeing him in other places just like the rest of us. And it's getting worse. If—"

"Danny, I'm not the one who wanted to crack this thing, okay? You wanted me to help and I'm trying to do that." Nelle lowered her voice, almost sultry in the static hum of the phone line. "Haven't you wanted to tell anyone else?"

Jordan and I exchanged glances, a tacit understanding between friends. Yes, we'd wanted to tell others. Danny, too. Another effect of the footage, perhaps—a desire to spread it around. Whether to inflict the dead man's presence on others or to help shoulder the burden, I'll never know.

"That's my point," Danny said. "We don't know what's going to happen. We don't even know what's really happening to us."

Nelle laughed. "It's obvious, isn't it? I thought you were smart, Danny. We're being haunted."

That word, "haunted," was something we'd all considered privately but didn't have the stones to voice. Seems fitting to me that Nelle would be the one to call it out—she had more guts than any of us—and her revelation raised the stakes in our madness to another level. We were being haunted by the ghost of a dead man. There, it's out. Now, what could we do about it?

For the first time since the call began, I spoke up. "We saw something we weren't supposed to see, guys. I don't know where this is going. I don't know how to stop it. But I think that if we're going to figure it out, we need to learn more about this tape."

Jordan chimed in: "It's like . . . you know when an outbreak occurs? We need to find the vector. The point of origin. Patient Zero. Whatever. You guys know what I mean."

Silence on the line. We did know. Clarence Duncan was the vector. Now to find someone who could point us in the right direction.

"Fine," Danny said. "If you think Brandon can help us . . ."

"Good." The victory in Nelle's voice was palpable, saccharine sweet. "I sent him the video last night."

She hung up, and Danny slammed the phone back on its cradle. Jordan walked upstairs to check on his brother, but I remained in the den, staring at the blank computer monitor. One thing troubled me most, something no one else acknowledged—or maybe they were afraid to: Clarence Duncan killed himself, and we were dreaming of doing the same.

∎ STOP

July 6th, 2016

Jordan invited me to church last weekend. The invitation was so unexpected that I didn't know what to say other than "thanks" and "yes, I'll go." I don't know why I did. God and I haven't seen eye to eye in a long time, but whatever. It meant a lot to J.

I got dressed up for the first time in years. Walked downstairs to stand on the corner. His car slows down, pulls along the curb, and I open the door to climb inside. J takes one look at me and his face goes pale. He stammers, tells me to get the fuck out of his car, and I'm barely out of the car before he's speeding away.

Later that night, he texts me and asks me to forgive him. Says that when I started to sit down, he saw Hardy's face instead of mine. He skipped church, drove home and took an extra dose of his meds.

He texts and says he loves me but doesn't think we should meet up anymore. It's better that way.

Fucked up thing is, I agree with him. Robby had the right idea, moving away and cutting ties. We're reminders of what happened. Each of us, to each other. The dead man is with us forever.

‖ PAUSE

DANNY'S DESPAIR IN this entry is difficult to read, and in the hours since I began this testament to our futility, I've unearthed a regret I thought I'd buried deep. Danny and Jordan were probably the best friends I ever had. Recounting the last few weeks before everything changed has been a form of torture unique to the circumstances; with every memory, I find myself thinking of what I should've done, what I could've done differently. Mostly, I think about the friendships we damaged.

I remember the last time I talked to Danny was in college, when I ran into him outside a bar in downtown Lexington. He was drunk and crying in the rain, and he asked if I had any pills to help him sleep. I shrugged him off and told him to go home. Don't think me lacking in compassion—I would've helped him if I could trust him, but the last time I let him crash at my place, he stole money from my wallet to score drugs.

I'd coped with the occasional sightings of Mr. Hardy with therapy, prescription drugs, and a healthy dose of artistic catharsis. I sought a professional to tell me the ghost was in my head, a manifestation of deeper maladies, and during my college years, I was able to carve out a life. Danny had trouble adjusting after what happened in our hometown and still insisted on trying to find a way to escape Hardy. He'd already experimented with drugs during our freshman year, pot and shrooms mostly—the harmless stuff—but by our second year, he'd escalated to oxy.

Jordan and I tried to intervene, and Danny swore he'd get clean, but his attempt at rehab lasted all of one week before he checked himself out. He dropped out of school afterward but remained in Lexington, crashing on Jordan's couch until he could get back on his feet, which would always happen for a month or two before he'd relapse and lose whatever job he'd acquired. I won't mince words—Danny had a rough go of things, and up until the end, he was still trying to find meaning in Hardy's curse. If he could find a reason, he could find the means to stop what was happening to us.

I'd like to think he went down fighting until Hardy got the best of him, but I know better.

▶ PLAY

We met Nelle and Brandon in the parking lot after school the next day. Until that day, I'd never spoken to him directly. He was always this presence on the opposite side of the room, both of us traveling parallel through high school.

I wasn't impressed. Black jeans, chains dangling from his pockets, a ripped Marilyn Manson T-shirt, and a leather bracelet with spiked studs—everything about him screamed "I'm edgy." I didn't take him seriously, and once he sensed my ambivalence, we were forever at odds with one another.

Our plan that day was to drive into Breyersburg together and talk to Brandon's uncle at Video Fantastique. After viewing Hardy's suicide, Brandon insisted on being the one to introduce us.

"He'll know you're serious if I'm with you," he said, unlocking the door to his van. "The Doom Mobile," as he called it, was a hulk of rusted metal that predated all of us and had seen far better days. A flourish of spray paint clung to the van's passenger side, a black and white monstrosity intended to resemble the Misfits skull logo. Jordan was the only one brave enough to call it out.

"Why do you have a weird clown on your van?"

Brandon glared at him while we shoegazed and stifled laughter. "Get in the van, losers."

Nelle hopped into the passenger seat, a move which disturbed Danny and I, but we kept our mouths shut. Jordan opened the van's backdoors and revealed a cavern of guitar cases, fast food wrappers, and a few milk crates to serve as seating. The van smelled like feet.

Brandon looked at us in the rearview. "Hold on to something. The suspension in this beast is shot."

He wasn't lying. The fifteen-mile drive to Breyersburg was agonizing and would've been even without the van's lack of shock absorption. Brandon insisted on blasting his band's demo tape at full volume, a screeching drop-tuned mess backed by a tone-deaf singer. They called themselves Dahmer's Appetite. They were as bad as you might imagine.

Nelle didn't seem to mind, though. She bobbed her head to the beat with an enthusiasm we'd never seen from her before. In between songs, Brandon cracked jokes about his bandmates and the local competition—Imbalance, Shotgun XII, The Yellow Kings—and Nelle laughed at every one of them. We couldn't get there fast enough, and halfway through the fourth song lovingly titled "The Cold Left Tit of a Dead Nun," Brandon slowed the van and pulled off the highway.

Video Fantastique occupied multiple storefronts in a single strip mall, its latter half serving as a massive storage area for Mr. Helmford's extensive collection. The shop's main retail space contained just about every VHS release, from obscure bootleg copies of Troma films to the most popular tripe pouring out of Hollywood. We're talking wall-to-wall racks of VHS cassettes, with random bins full of cassettes marked "buy one, get one free." There was even a small Betamax section. Any free wall space was papered in movie posters, demonstrating an obsession with all things celluloid and magnetic tape. I wouldn't be surprised if Video Fantastique was the south's largest VHS depository in its day.

Thomas Helmford sat behind the register, his bespectacled eyes glued to the small TV on the counter, while munching absently from a bag of chips. He looked up when the doorbell chimed to announce our entrance.

"Didn't expect you until the weekend, Brando." Thomas crumpled the bag of chips and wiped the oil from his hands. "Who're your friends?" He adjusted his glasses and took us in. "*New* friends, I take it?"

"Not exactly," Brandon said. He put his arm around Nelle, and I caught Danny's glare from the corner of my eye. "This here's Nelle. And these guys, well . . . " He dismissed us with a wave of his hand. "They're Nelle's friends."

Nelle's friends. I rolled my eyes and stepped forward. "We're here to ask you about a rare VHS tape."

"That so? Well, I've been known to acquire rare

tapes from time to time." He looked us over again. "If it's a porno, I'll need to see some ID—"

"It's not like that," Danny said. He'd been quiet since we'd left school, lost in his head, running away from the storm brewing there. His dry voice was a rude wake-up call, a reminder of the dire situation in which we found ourselves. "You ever heard of something called the Duncan Tape?"

Mr. Helmford chuckled, shook his head. "Where'd you hear about that?" He glared at Brandon. "What did I tell you about staying away from this weird shit? If your mom finds out, she'll fuckin' skin me alive, kid."

"Sir," Jordan said, "we really just need some information. It's important. Please."

Thomas sighed. He plucked his glasses from his face and began cleaning the lenses with his sleeve. "Important, huh? Sure, kid. Follow me."

▶ FAST FWD

Thomas led us into the store's storage room. "Storage" was an understatement. We passed entire sections dedicated to vintage porn, old concert bootleg videos, recordings of sporting events, and stacks of unmarked cassettes. At the opposite end of the room was a series of television sets of varying sizes and accompanying VCR units, a work table littered with soldering tools and wires, a Sony PlayStation and Nintendo 64, and several cabinet speakers. Thomas plopped down into an oversized office chair and spun to face us like a comic book villain.

"You have any idea how many people have come

to me asking about the Duncan Tape?" We looked at one another, hesitant to speak. Thomas saved us the trouble. "It's rhetorical. No one has ever asked me about the Duncan Tape. Do you know why? Because it doesn't exist."

Everyone looked at me. That feeling, like you've been called on by a teacher when you're not paying attention? It felt like that, except it was much worse. I shook my head, my words tripping over one another in a rush of explanation.

"It's all an urban legend, kid. Everyone's heard the stories of that tape. A congressman kills himself on camera, and then the cameraman tries to get rich by selling a copy of the broadcast. He then kills himself because . . . what, the dead congressman made him do it? He was depressed? Come on, guys. It's all *X-Files* horseshit."

"But it *is* true," I said. "Clarence Duncan worked at the station, and he did kill himself."

"Right, sure. So what? There's no proof he made a tape of the suicide. There's no proof he sold it to anyone. There's no proof he killed himself under dubious circumstances. The only proof any of us have is a dead congressman and a dead cameraman." Thomas spun in his chair, gestured to the array of TVs. "I've seen thousands of tapes, guys. Literally thousands. I've got a copy of the Zapruder film, a copy of Monroe riding DiMaggio raw-dog, eye-witness footage of UFO sightings and other mystical mumbo jumbo. I've been doin' this for nearly a decade, and I ain't never seen a video of a congressman killing himself. If it existed, I would've seen it. It's a myth, kid."

Nelle spoke up for the first time since our arrival. I'd like to think she sensed my defeat and was coming to my rescue. The glance she gave me when she stepped forward said as much, and so did the flutter in my belly.

"But we have proof."

Thomas crossed his arms and smirked. "That so, little lady?"

"Yes, and don't call me 'little lady' unless I can call you 'sexist pig.' Deal?"

Silence in the warehouse save for the electric hum of blank TV screens. Dark splotches of red blossomed on Thomas's cheeks. He cleared his throat.

"Fair enough. Can you show it to me?"

"I sent it to Brandon. He can send it to you."

"Well, all right then." Thomas turned, looked up at Brandon, and swatted the boy's arm with a copy of *Consumer Electronics*. "Next time, pick up the phone and call me first, you dipshit."

■ S T O P

▷ PLAY

July 30th, 2016

Couldn't sleep. Too much on my mind. Got
served an eviction notice. Gonna move
back to Stauford. I'm not in love with
the idea, but I've got nowhere else I can
go. ~~Maybe I can make a new start of
things.~~

   Bullshit. There are no new starts for
me. Wish I could rewind this horror film,
but that ain't happening. All I can do is
hit Play and keep the tape rolling.

   Had the dream again. If that's not
an omen, I don't know what is. I was in

the conference room, surrounded by an audience of my friends wearing Hardy's face. Same as always—I ramble for a minute and then I put a gun in my mouth. Same as everyone else. I don't know if J or Robby still have the dreams, but I'm willing to bet they do. Don't know how we've lasted this long. Sometimes I think the dead man is just toying with us, you know? Because we were the ones who downloaded that video and watched it first. He's saved us for last.

Sometimes I dream about other things, though.

Sometimes I dream about Nelle. It's funny, you know, the way we can still dream about people we haven't seen or thought about in years. Like they're still alive somewhere inside us, going about their business, and sometimes they make themselves known. Sometimes they say what we've always wanted them to say. Sometimes we have a chance to say what we wish we'd said.

Sometimes I dream about sweet Nelle. It's just the two of us in class, and she says she wants to tell me a secret. I lean in, ask her to whisper it to me, and she kisses me on the cheek. That's her secret, and now it's mine, and that's the dream. Just a kiss, but to me it means everything, good and bad.

My dreams make me feel foolish, you know. Because there's a moment after waking when I'm still lost in the fog, when I think everything's okay and the way things were before are how they are now.

But the fog always clears. Reality always hits me like a hammer, and I spend ten minutes sobbing into my pillow because I know the way things were will never be again. The dead man's face is still there, watching me from a window or a TV screen or a computer monitor or ~~from anyone~~ else on the street. And he's not the only one haunting me now. The days I dream of Nelle are the days she haunts me too.

■ S T O P

I'VE HAD A difficult time reading some of these entries, but this passage finally broke me. What happened to Nelle hit us hard, but none harder than Danny, and that was the beginning of the end of our friendship. He blamed me and he had every right to. I blame myself. If I hadn't told her about the video, she wouldn't have grown obsessed with it.

Sometimes I wonder why she was the first, why we were passed over, and in this respect, I agree with Danny: the dead man was toying with us. Torturing us. Punishing us for digging up his grave. What better way to hurt the living than to make them lose everything they love and deny them death?

Maybe it was Nelle's attachment to the video that drew Hardy's ire. If we'd dug up his grave, Nelle had danced with his corpse. Worse yet, she'd made him speak.

◀◀REWIND

After the incident at Video Fantastique, we returned to Stanford and went our separate ways for about a week. I still had lunch with Danny and Jordan, but Nelle made herself scarce from our daily meetings. We still chatted on ICQ, but her messages and times online were sporadic at best. A lack of sleep slowly took its toll on her as it had on us, but after several days, her exhaustion grew far more apparent. She went to school wearing the same clothes, her hair unwashed, and she stopped doing her homework. Our chemistry teacher, Mr. Hart, pulled her aside one day, and I overheard him ask if there was something going on at home. Nelle looked through him, shook her head. "Just depressed," she mumbled. "I'm taking medication." I never got a chance to ask her if that was true. She hadn't just distanced herself from us, but from Brandon as well—who, I must add, wasn't looking too great himself.

Everywhere I went, teachers and students alike asked if I was sick. Why wouldn't they? I looked like I had a horrible case of the flu—pale skin, swollen red eyes, the fatigued gait of someone who hasn't slept in days. I lost my motivation to do anything except the most basic of routines. Getting out of bed was a milestone achievement. My hygiene suffered, showers took too much effort, and by the end of the week, my forehead was pockmarked with acne. Mom was so busy with her jobs that we rarely saw each other, so she didn't notice my descent into . . . depression? Malaise? I don't know what else to call it. It's like I was slowly being drained of life, or at the very least, drained of my will to be.

Going to work wasn't any better. You'd think the

mundane bustle of Walmart on a weeknight would take my mind off things, something to keep me occupied. But the sad truth is, pushing shopping carts for several hours is anything but mentally stimulating. And Hardy wasn't about to let me forget his demise regardless of my occupation. One night, while on my way to clock out, I noticed Hardy's bloody face on the row of display TVs in Electronics. I stopped in the aisle, unable to move, staring down a dozen iterations of his grim visage. Movie trailers, football commercials, a Walmart promo featuring Sam Walton himself—Hardy was in them all, watching with the same cold, bloody indifference. I wanted to smash every screen and erase his horrible face, and I might've done it if not for my need of the job. Instead, I forced myself to look away, and made a beeline for the employee lounge. I avoided the Electronics department after that.

Danny and Jordan weren't any better. As the days crawled by, we met at lunch and after school but spoke little. Our communication was clear in our appearance and body language, a silent understanding between friends: we were in a bad place, and none of us knew how to get out of it. I remember thinking how silly it was that we were all suffering from watching the video of a man kill himself. "Silly," a word only a stupid teenager would use to describe the visceral finality of suicide. I thought I knew everything when I was seventeen, but in hindsight, looking back on these painful moments, I know now that I knew nothing. Silly me.

One night the following week, I received a message from Nelle over ICQ. "Meet me tomorrow at lunch" was all it said. She'd already signed off so I couldn't reply. A quick check with Danny confirmed he'd received the same message. I thought about calling Nelle to make sure she was okay, but I didn't follow through. I wish I had. I want to believe it might've changed things, but more probably it wouldn't have changed anything. I know that now.

▶ PLAY

Hardy paid me another visit the next morning. I stood in our tiny kitchen, looking through the cabinets for a box of cereal, when Mom shuffled past me in search of her keys. She was supposed to have the day off, and I said as much while moving from one cabinet to the next.

"Mr. Stone called and asked me to work a double. We need the money."

I looked away from the cabinet, intending to tell her she deserved one day off, and the dead man's face stole the words from my throat. There he was, standing in my kitchen, looking ridiculous in my mom's cardigan. His face stuttered and glitched, the features fuzzy and hissing with static. I gaped at my mother—at *him*—while she went about her business, rummaging through her purse and mumbling to herself. Hardy's face turned toward me when she found her keys. Blood seeped out of his nose and over his bulbous bottom lip, pouring over his chin and vanishing from the air. He glitched, and for a split second I saw my mother's face through the interference. She was still there, staring at me and wondering what was wrong.

"Rob?"

"Yeah, Mom?"

"Is it my hair? Did I mess up my mascara?" She stuck her hand into her purse for a compact mirror. Benjamin Hardy's cloudy eyes drifted up and stared at me. "Something in my teeth? You're making me nervous."

I forced myself to look away, closed my eyes, took a breath and counted to five.

"Rob? What's wrong?"

"Nothing, Mom. I . . . was going to tell you something, but I forgot what it was."

When I looked back, she was herself again. Hardy was gone. Mom reached out, put her hand on my forehead. "Well, you're not warm." She pulled me close for a hug. "You just look like you're coming down with something. Call me if you need me, okay?"

I told her I would, and she kissed my forehead. Minutes later, she was out the door, and I held myself together until I saw her car leave the trailer park. The tears came after, and the tremors after that. I remember that morning so well because it's the first time I was ever truly terrified. I'd seen him before, sure, but seeing him again drove home the certainty that he would never leave me. That certainty fueled a hopelessness I'd not experienced before. What kid truly comprehends the inevitability of death? Not me, not then.

It's that moment when your blood turns to ice, your heart plunges to hell, and you find yourself staring beyond the veil into the cold dark nothing waiting for us all. Most people find themselves facing that stark nothingness on the verge of death, when all systems are shutting down and the lights are beginning to dim. A few of us are lucky and never see it coming. And those of us who downloaded a stupid video one night in 1998 gained the knowledge of death far too young. When we peered beyond the veil, we saw more than the peace of nonexistence. We saw a dead man's visage waiting to usher us over the threshold. Waiting for us to join him. Nelle was right: we were being haunted.

Later that day, I met my friends for lunch in our usual spot. Nelle was already there waiting for us, and she looked like shit. Beyond the bloodshot eyes and unwashed hair, she had a series of scratches all along her chin and throat. I sat next to her, watched her from the corner of my eye.

"You watched it again, didn't you?"

"How'd you know?"

"Because you look worse than we do."

She snorted, forced a smile. "You know how to win a girl's heart." Danny and Jordan sat across from us, and we ate our lunches in silence until Nelle pushed away her tray. "Yeah, I watched it again. Several times."

Danny looked up from his meal. "You said you wouldn't."

"I know what I said. I didn't—I couldn't help it. It was just there, and I had to see it again. I don't know, it's too weird to explain. Like . . . watching it again might make me feel better, you know?"

We all grunted in agreement. Jordan told me a few days before that he caught Danny with the video player open on the screen. The mouse cursor hovered over the Play icon. His brother was in a sort of trance, staring at the blank image, tears dribbling from frozen eyes. Jordan said he couldn't get mad, because he'd felt the desire to do it too.

And so did I. How many times had I thought about messaging Danny to request the video? Too many. A shitty modem and a single phone line were all that kept me from doing it. Mom would've grounded me from the internet if she knew I'd tied up the phone all night.

But I still thought about it, and often at night while trying to fall asleep. The thought of seeing it again brought a weird sense of comfort to me. Like witnessing Hardy's death again might reinvigorate me, free me from this depressive state I'd been trapped in since we watched the video. I know, it doesn't make sense, but that was the weird intoxicating power of the video. Once it got in your head, you couldn't stop thinking about it, even if visions of the victim on screen haunted you for the rest of your days.

"Anyway," Nelle said, "I want you guys to help me with something. I want to contact him. My dad's got one of those Ouija boards."

Silence fell over us as Nelle's intentions sank in. Jordan put his fork down and considered her words as he chewed his food. Danny wasn't as contemplative.

"You're serious?"

"I am."

"Nelle, even if that would work, what the hell would you hope to accomplish?"

"I don't know. Do you have any better ideas? *Fuck.*"

71

She shouted that last word, earning the attention of our peers from the next table over.

"Keep it down," Jordan hissed. "Shit. You want us all to get detention?"

She ignored him. "I want to know why he's doing this, Danny. I want him to stop. I haven't had a good night's sleep in weeks. He's in my head, in my dreams, he's on my mom's face, he's on my TV, my computer. I can't do anything without him breathing down my goddamn neck, and I'm tired of it." Nelle wiped her eyes with her sleeve. "But he's all I can think about. I see that look in his eyes after he pulled the trigger. I've watched it so many times, guys. You can kind of see when the lights go out for him, the second that bullet pierces his brain—"

"Nelle," Danny said, "please stop."

"—and there's a moment where it's like his soul leaves his body and gets trapped in the screen. You've seen it. We've all seen it, and we didn't even know it. You have to slow the video down and go frame by frame. There's a shadow that leaves his head, gets tangled in the grain and scanlines. Looks like smoke which is probably why no one noticed—"

"Nelle!" Danny slammed his hand on the table so hard our trays rattled. The cafeteria fell silent, and the algebra teacher, Mrs. Johnson, stood up from the teachers' table. She walked to our side of the room and crossed her arms.

"There a problem over here, Mr. Chambers?"

Danny glared at Nelle, who stared solemnly at her tray of half-eaten food. His cheeks flushed red, matched the color of his eyes.

"No, Mrs. Johnson."

Mrs. Johnson looked at Nelle. "And you, Ms. Simmons?"

Nelle lifted her chin, opened her mouth to speak, and froze. I did the same. So did Danny and Jordan. Benjamin Hardy's dead face gazed down on us all. Grainy monochromatic blood flickered and faded from his distorted face. His appearance took us all by surprise, and we took turns spouting a litany of expletives out of pure fright. Jordan shot out of his chair and backed against the wall. Nelle tried to stand, caught her foot against the table leg, and fell backward. She landed hard on the tile with a sharp cry. I jumped from my seat and knelt beside Nelle to see if she was okay. Danny remained at the table, frozen in fear as Mrs. Johnson's voice spoke from behind the dead man's bloody maw.

"What is wrong with you kids? You know better than to use that kind of language. Detention, all of you."

The cafeteria murmured collectively, our peers watching as we collected ourselves and returned to our seats. We finished our meals in silence, and when the bell rang, Nelle told us she'd meet us at Danny's house that evening.

I don't remember much else about that day, except that detention was painfully boring. The dead man didn't make another appearance—at least not to me, and if my friends saw him, they never said. Two things stand out to me about the lunch room incident: it was the first time I'd ever earned afternoon detention, and there were others who saw the man's face on Mrs. Johnson. I didn't realize it until much later when the damage was done. Whole tables of students stared at her, their expressions of fatigue and terror unmistakable. Some of them looked like they hadn't slept in days.

Some of them looked like they'd seen a ghost.

‖ PAUSE

I admit Nelle's plan was hokey. All we knew about Ouija boards was what Hollywood taught us. Want demons? Use a Ouija board and invite them into your life. Only bad things happen when a Ouija board is involved. You don't know who you're talking to with the board, you can't close the doors you open, and so on. Like I said: hokey.

None of us were religious, at least not in the way our grandparents were. Aside from Jordan's born-again direction in recent years, we were all as agnostic as they come, especially given the time and the area in which we grew up. We were old enough that our parents couldn't force us to go to church, and none of us wanted to, anyway. The people who picked on us every day, called us names, bullied us every school year were the ones who went to church. Central Baptist in downtown Stauford was where all the hypocrites and sycophants went to jerk each other off on Sundays.

Looking back, I'd like to think we were too smart for religion—at least, we believed we were. Our generation was too caught up in the moment, living day to day and minute to minute while riding this new, exciting wave called the internet. Who has time to think about the afterlife when the latest mod for *Quake 2* is available for download?

Generation Y, Millenials, whatever we were, we

weren't concerned about ancient doctrine or philosophy. Angels and devils were stories told to give us hope or scare us. All we wanted was to live, man, and enjoy our time while we could, come whatever may. Music was great, movies and games were great, and we couldn't wait to graduate and leave our shitty little town. The horrors of 9/11 hadn't happened yet, the economy hadn't collapsed, and a gallon of gas cost less than a buck-ten. The millennium was coming up. The threat of Y2K was real and yet no one understood why. College was on the horizon, the gateway to our successful futures, and what an exciting time that promised to be.

Who had time for ghosts and the words of dead men? Why worry about superstitious dangers? How many cracks have I stepped on without breaking Mom's back? I've lost count of how many black cats have crossed my path. We—I—grew up in a time when none of that mattered because tomorrow was a million years away. Even now, as my peers are back home living with their parents, unable to afford what society promised them twenty years ago, we're all still living day to day. Living in the moment. We have no time for superstition because, hey, I need to meet my hourly quota for the day, week, month so I can pay my bills and continue surviving.

So, yeah, when I think about what we did with the Ouija board that night, I can't help but feel indifferent to the implications. We were just trying to survive the day, while something we didn't understand slowly leeched our will from us.

We were seventeen and stupid, with no concept of what we were dealing with.

All we wanted was to live.

▶ PLAY

Nelle arrived at Danny's house around eight that evening. Jordan smoothed things over with their parents, telling them we all had a group project for school. Which wasn't a lie, not really. Benjamin Hardy was our morbid group project, just not for school. The stakes were much higher.

We didn't dim the lights and we didn't waste time with candles. No one had sage on hand to burn just in case, and we didn't pour salt in the doorways and on the window panes. It was just the four of us in the den, scattered on the carpet with an old Ouija board in front of us. The planchette was light and made of plastic.

"This is stupid."

Danny wasn't wrong. I felt foolish even looking at the board and its arrangement of letters and numbers. YES and NO in opposite corners, GOOD BYE at the bottom. Nelle placed the planchette in the center. Jordan looked at her, curious.

"You ever do this before?"

"Once," she said. "When I was a kid. Me and my cousins tried it."

"Anything happen?"

Nelle smirked. "The lights went out. Scared the shit out of us. Turns out my mom tripped the breaker when she ran the blender. She was trying to make us milkshakes."

I watched her place her fingers on the planchette. "You don't think this will work?"

She looked at me, smiled. "I don't know. I hope so.

I didn't believe in ghosts until I watched the video. Did any of you?" We shook our heads. "Come on," Nelle whispered. "We all need to do this."

Danny sighed, placed his fingers on the planchette. Jordan followed. I went last, resting my fingertips on the cheap piece of plastic.

Nelle closed her eyes, breathed deep, and mumbled something under her breath that sounded like "please." Then she raised her voice and said, "Benjamin Hardy, we're calling out to you. We demand to know what you want from us."

Silence. From upstairs, the muffled voice of a talking head on the news. Ron and Debra Chambers talking about work. A slow drip from a bathroom faucet. Outside, wind blowing dead leaves across the driveway.

My stomach gurgled. Jordan scratched his nose to hold back a sneeze. Danny shook his head, took his hand off the planchette.

"Nelle, I'm sorry, but this is silly. It's—"

"Benjamin Hardy," she went on, "you owe us an explanation. Answer us. Answer me."

The planchette twitched beneath our fingers, and we gasped from the sensation. Nelle hissed at Danny, told him to put his fingers back on the surface. He obeyed.

"What do you want from us?"

Slowly, the planchette inched across the board, charting a course between letters. O-T-H-E-R-S.

"Are you doing this, D?" Jordan cracked a smile, expecting his brother to admit to the joke, but Danny wasn't laughing. None of us were. The planchette moved on its own. Only Nelle was fearless—or desperate—enough to continue the conversation. The rest of us would've stopped there if we could.

"Is this Benjamin Hardy?"

The planchette slid to the corner: NO.

"Who are you?"

I-A-M-Y-O-U.

We looked at each other, confused. Nelle asked again, "Is this Benjamin Hardy?" The planchette didn't move. I suggested she ask a different question, but Nelle shook her head.

"Who are we speaking to?"

Y-O-U-R-F-A-C-E-I-S-M-Y-F-A-C-E.

"Answer me, goddammit."

"Nelle," Danny said softly. He put his hand on her shoulder. "This isn't going anywhere. Calm down."

She slapped his hand away, her weary eyes poised on the board. Jordan and I removed our hands from the planchette and moved away to give her space.

Danny appealed to her once more. "Nelle, please—"

"I have to stop it, Danny. Don't you understand that?" She looked at me and Jordan. "Don't any of you understand that? Do you see what it's doing to me? To us?" Nelle was trapped in a web of desperation, a web of her own making. A web we would all spin for ourselves sooner or later. She wiped her eyes and continued: "What do you want from me, Benjamin?"

O-T-H-E-R-S.

"I don't understand. What others?" She looked at each of us. "The guys? Danny and Jordan and Robby?"

The planchette moved to the corner of the board: NO. Once the planchette settled on its answer, it shot off the board with the force of a hockey puck and struck the far wall. From behind us came the familiar warbling noise of a degaussing screen. I turned and watched the computer monitor flicker to life. A desktop wallpaper of Jenny McCarthy came into focus, but her features were wrong. She was bloated, her skin graying and peeling like old paint, and her face sagged until her gums and eye sockets were exposed. Blood oozed from her nostrils and elongated mouth.

I cleared my throat. "Guys . . ."

We watched in shocked silence as the image deteriorated in real time, Jenny McCarthy's once slender features bloating and slowly decomposing into digital noise. Benjamin Hardy's face emerged from a pool of black static. A single word hissed from the computer speakers: "Others." The voice was unmistakable, even with the distortion and gurgling interference of air through liquid. Hardy's voice came through loud and clear.

"Someone turn it off," Jordan said. He looked to his brother. "Turn it off, D."

Danny was halfway across the room when something popped inside the computer case, and the screen went dark. A thin stream of smoke rose from

the corner of the disc drive. Both brothers scrambled **to their** computer, panicking over the apparent hardware failure, and I remember turning to Nelle to gauge her reaction. She sat with her knees drawn up to her chin. Tears welled in her eyes.

I called her name, and when she looked up at me, I lost the words of reassurance. Nothing I could say would've alleviated the utter loss in her eyes.

In the weeks following everything that went down at Brandon's house, authorities ruled there was no planning involved. The event was spontaneous, with one person's actions fueling the next, not entirely dissimilar from the so-called Werther Effect, but on a much smaller and immediate scale.

I think Nelle knew what she was going to do before she did it. Thinking back, recalling that look in her eye, I've no doubt about that.

She knew.

■ S T O P

▷ PLAY

October 18th, 2016

Haven't written since I moved home to Stauford. Got an apartment in that complex at the foot of Gordon Hill. Someone built a radio station up there near the old water tower. An actual rock station. Me and J and Rob used to bitch all the time about the shitty radio choices in town. Country or gospel or Top 40 garbage. This was years before the satellite stations. I've got the station playing right now. It keeps me company in the night. The late-night

DJ, Cindy-something, she's got a hell of a voice.

I'm waffling. I don't want to write about what I'm supposed to write about. Told my therapist I'd keep this up, and I'm going to do my best.

The town hasn't changed since I was here last. Been a few years, and longer since I lived here. Too many memories. ~~Too many that I don't want to think about. Too many reminders.~~

No. I'll face this. I'll put this down, and then I'll try to get back to sleep.

I went for a drive the other day, no real destination in mind, just an evening journey to get lost and find my way back again. Ended up out on the parkway, halfway between Stauford and Breyersburg. Decided to keep going, just to see what they did with the video store. It's an empty lot now. Nothing there but weeds and dirt, an empty rectangle between shops in the strip mall. Video Fantastique, indeed.

I circled around, pulled off the side of the road and looked at the empty space. Realtor signs litter the perimeter. Whoever owns it now is trying to sell the whole complex. Good luck getting asking price. Makes me wonder if they have to disclose what happened here. The owner's suicide. The arson. All those video tapes went up like the Hindenburg.

Sometimes I think about that night. The chaos of it all.

Robby was so terrified someone would call the cops and identify his car, but they never did. Still can't believe he lit the match—you never know what your friends can do until they do it. Sometimes you've got them figured out, and other times, well, they'll surprise you.

Robby did.

He set fire to that place without hesitation, and I don't blame him at all.

I'm kind of ~~proud~~ of him for doing it. I just wish I'd been there to help him do it.

‖ P A U S E

▮▮ IDEO FANTASTIQUE BURNED to the ground on the night of Saturday, October 24th, 1998. Investigators ruled it negligence on the part of its owner, Thomas Helmford, whose remains were found among the cinders. The county coroner ruled Helmford's death a suicide, courtesy of a charred revolver found in his hand. In Helmford's haste to end his life, he'd left a cigarette burning near an open VHS cassette he was attempting to repair. The film caught fire, investigators said, and spread to the massive collection contained in the store's warehouse. Helmford was already dead when the flames consumed him.

That last part is true. He was dead when the fire started. The rest, however, is grossly inaccurate.

So. Full disclosure: I started the fire. I've done a lot of stupid things in my life. I regret them all except for one act of arson.

I'd do it again if given the chance.

◄◄ R E W I N D

The Ouija incident left us all shaken and more confused **than before**. Nelle quietly left Danny's house while he and Jordan mourned their dead computer. She was already backing out of the driveway when I noticed she was gone. I thought about chasing after her, but I didn't know what to say, so I didn't. I wish I had.

Back in the den, Danny and Jordan diagnosed the problem with their computer. The hard drive was fried. Jordan burned his fingers unplugging the drive from the motherboard, and we spent a few minutes marveling at the charred metal casing.

I asked if they'd ever seen something like this before. Danny looked at me, pale-faced and wide-eyed. "No."

"We had a surge once," Jordan said, rubbing his fingertips. "Fried everything. It's all connected in there. But just one piece? No way."

"But there wasn't—" I began, but Danny cut me off.

"No surge. I know." He looked at the blank monitor. "It was *him*."

This whole time, Danny hadn't spoken of Hardy with a context of sentience. Hardy was always past-tense, a suicide statistic, and until that moment, I don't think Danny truly faced the possibility of what we were dealing with. The air in the room had weight, thick with the stench of ozone and gunpowder, and after further tinkering, we all retreated upstairs to the front porch.

The autumn air was refreshing, and I remember breathing it in, holding it as long as I could. I felt alive. I *needed* to feel alive. All this business with Hardy's digital remains left me feeling empty inside.

Jordan broke the silence with a quiet chuckle. "Well," he said, "at least the file's gone."

"Along with our games, our music . . ." Danny buried his head in his hands. "How are we going to explain this to Dad?"

We were back to worrying about replacing expensive hardware and the software we'd accumulated over the years. Worse, what would happen when the parental units found out? Real teenager concerns. No talk of suicide or a dead congressman or dissecting a mystery behind a video. Just three seventeen-year-olds stressing over something trivial. The way things should've been.

Now that I think about it, that was probably our last night as teenagers. Everything that came after catapulted us into the stark reality of adulthood, that grim wasteland of accountability and repercussions. We weren't ready for it, even if we thought we were. Shit, is anyone?

▶ P L A Y

The next day was a Friday. October 23rd, if we're keeping score.

Nelle didn't show, and I don't think any of us were surprised by that. Her outward health had deteriorated significantly in the last several weeks, and even if she wasn't sick, convincing an adult wouldn't be difficult. Danny and Jordan kept to themselves most of the day. When we sat together at lunch, little was spoken between us. What else could be said? We were all subject to something none of us truly understood, something we couldn't go to our parents about, and something that any doctor would diagnose as a mental health disorder. We were alone in this.

Or so we thought.

I stopped by my locker after lunch to drop off some books. While standing there, I heard a familiar voice from the other side of the row.

"—it's the most fucked up thing I've ever seen."

"You swear it's legit?"

"Oh yeah, totally legit. Way more intense than those shitty *Faces of Death* videos. You can see the guy's brains on the wall."

"How much?"

"Fifty."

"I dunno, man. That's pretty steep."

"I didn't tell you the best part. It changes every time you watch it."

Silence for a moment, and then: "You're bullshitting me."

"Honest. You'll see something different every time. Hell, you'll see things even when you aren't watching it."

"Still, fifty bucks, man . . . "

"Tell you what. My parents are out of town so I'm throwing a little viewing party at my place tomorrow night. You come by, see it for yourself. Decide then if you want the video."

"Wow, thanks." A beat. "But . . . why would I want to buy it if I've already seen it?"

"Trust me. It's the sort of thing you want to watch over and over. Like it gets in your head. It's all you'll think about."

"Right on. I'll see you tomorrow night, man."

I closed my locker and turned the corner just in time to see some sophomore kid walking away from Brandon Helmford. The goth wannabe held a black VHS cassette case. I walked up to him and snatched it from his hand.

"What the fuck, man?"

"You goddamn idiot." I opened the case, took out the VHS tape. A handwritten label read "Duncan Tape" above the Video Fantastique logo. "What the hell do you think you're doing?"

Brandon grabbed the video and pushed me away. "Free country, free enterprise. Now fuck off."

"Nelle sent that to you in confidence. You piece of shit. How many copies did you make?"

"None of your business."

"You know what it does. Jesus, look in the mirror, dude."

A waste of breath. He knew what he looked like. Zits, pale skin, red and swollen eyes—he was losing as much sleep as the rest of us, if not more. Brandon shoved the video case into his locker and slammed the door.

"Leave me alone, nerd. I've got class."

"How many times did you watch it?" He ignored me, kept walking down the hall. "How many?"

He raised his hand and gave me the finger. "This many."

I watched him until he turned a corner and was gone. The bell rang, but I remained in the hall, watching other students rush off to class. How many of them had copies? How many could Thomas Helmford record in the weeks since Brandon sent him the video? Hundreds? Thousands? If the Duncan

Tape didn't exist before, it certainly did now for the low price of fifty bucks. Brandon was probably splitting the profit with his uncle.

My head swam with possibilities, all of them grim. I searched the faces of my classmates, looking for the signs of fatigue and malaise, but there were so many, and what teenager doesn't look tired or bored at school? I needed to find Danny and Jordan. I needed—

Cold sweat sheathed my skin as my heart raced. My vision doubled, and a loud drone filled my ears. I breathed deep and fast, struggling to keep myself together while the world slowly pulled me apart. I sank to my knees amid the between-class turmoil, and I don't remember who stopped to help me or who called for a teacher. The rest is a blur until the nurse's office.

Panic attack, they told me. My first, and not my last. They called my mom at work, suggested she check me out of school and take me home to rest. She arrived half an hour later, and then we were on our way home.

"What happened, honey?"

I tried to articulate it but stopped myself from revealing why. What could I say? Mom, I'm being haunted by a ghost and something horrible is going to happen to all of us? Instead, I told her I was worried about a math test. Couldn't seem to get the hang of it.

"Why didn't you say something, Rob? I could've hired you a tutor."

I let her worry and be a mother. We both knew she couldn't afford to hire a tutor.

When we arrived home, I told her I just needed to rest. I told her I'd be okay, to go back to work.

"Are you sure, honey? You've never been like this before, and you look so pale, and—"

"I'll be okay." I gave her a hug.

"When did you grow up? It happened too fast, didn't it?"

"It did." I kissed her forehead. "Go back to work. I'm going to sleep."

When she was gone, I connected to the internet and tried to reach Nelle on ICQ. She had her status set to Do Not Disturb, so my messages wouldn't alert her. I tried email next, asking if she knew about Brandon's tapes, or his party. I waited an hour. No reply.

Defeated, I crawled into bed and closed my eyes and tried to quiet the anxiety in my mind. Sleep found me, and for the first time in weeks, I slept without dreams or nightmares. No audience of bleeding faces, no lectern, no camera. Just blissful nothingness. A brief respite from the madness that had engulfed our lives. I miss that sleep. It's been nightmares ever since.

▶ PLAY

My boss gave me hell for calling off work. She didn't care all that much about my anxiety episode earlier that day, was more concerned about having a warm body to push shopping carts across a parking lot. I thanked her for understanding and hung up before she could respond.

I'd slept for most of the afternoon, and the sun

was setting when I woke up. Mom was still at work, so I dialed in to the network and checked my email. No response from Nelle.

Considering her state of mind, I thought about taking a drive to the other side of town where she lived but didn't want to seem like a creep. She was tough, a rebel girl. She was fine.

Instead, I called Danny's house. Jordan answered on the third ring.

"Hey, man. Are you okay? What happened?"

Jordan's concern was a welcome change. I told him about the panic attack, asked if I could stop by. "Need to talk to you and your brother. It's about Brandon."

An hour later, we sat in the den of the Chambers residence. The family computer lay in pieces on the desk like a dissected specimen. Danny looked longingly at its remains and shook his head.

"A hundred and sixty bucks to replace that drive."

"I could always get you a job pushing carts with me at Walmart."

He threw a pillow at my face. "I'm not that desperate yet. Anyway, what's this about Brandon?"

I told them about the conversation I'd overheard earlier that day and the copies of the video. When I'd finished, the brothers looked at one another and then back to me.

"Robby," Jordan said, "me and Danny talked about this earlier, after you checked out of school. Maybe it's a good thing our hard drive died, you know? Like, maybe we can move on from this?"

"I don't understand. You want to 'move on' from this?" I looked at Danny. "You know what that video can do. What it's done to us. You both do."

"So let's keep out of it," Danny said. "The video's gone. We can't watch it anymore. It's out of our hands now."

"Out of our hands?" I climbed to my feet, paced the room in frustration. Danny and Jordan had pissed me off over the years, but never like this. If watching the video for the first time was a wedge in our friendship, our conversation that night was the hammer. "This is our fault, guys. We let that video get out. We gave it to Nelle. We—"

Danny shot to his feet and stood in front of me. "You got Nelle involved."

"Because you wanted to know where it came from. You wanted to know why it existed."

"Guys—" Jordan stood between us. Danny pushed him away.

"No, J. He wants to point fingers, so let's point fingers. You told Nelle about it. She sent it to Brandon. Brandon sent it to his scumbag uncle. This is on you, Rob. Whatever happens, it's on you. We're out of it."

I'd never raised a hand against my friends, but I wanted to. God, I wanted to. "You're out of it, huh? You still seeing the dead guy?" I looked at Jordan. "Still dreaming about his bloody face?"

Jordan looked away from me. Danny shook his head. "They're just dreams, man."

"Dreams where you die. Dreams where you fucking kill yourself. We've had the same dream, Danny." One of their parents shuffled around upstairs, and I lowered my voice. "Dreams you've thought about acting out. Don't tell me you haven't."

Jordan sighed, returned to the couch. "I just wanted to see Jenna Jameson's tits."

"I'm not going to kill myself, Rob. Just because you've thought about it doesn't mean I have. If anyone here's got a reason to do it, it's you."

"What the fuck is that supposed to mean?"

"Nothing. Forget it." Danny turned away, was going to take a seat beside his brother, but I grabbed his shoulder and made him face me.

"What did you mean by that, Danny?" He didn't say anything, so I pushed him. "Spit it out, D. What's my reason for wanting to kill myself? Tell me how I'm supposed to feel, you're so fucking smart." I pushed him again, and this time he pushed back.

"Because you're never getting out of this town," he snapped. "You're too poor to go anywhere else. You're here so much, our parents might as well fucking adopt you. They feel sorry for you, you know."

I shut my mouth, stunned. He wasn't wrong. I lived in a rented trailer with a mother who could barely make ends meet. My grades weren't great. All Stauford had to offer me was a shitty retail job making barely above minimum wage. The town was a dead-end for people like me.

People like me. The thought drove home this harsh reality of Stauford's sons and daughters. Most of the people here were born with nothing, lived with little, and died with even less. Tiny blips in human history, offering nothing to the species except a chiseled marker saying "I was here for a time. Now I'm not."

Danny frowned, shook his head. "Rob, I didn't mean that."

"No," I said, wiping my eyes. "You did. Don't lie." I looked at Jordan and waved. "I'll see you later, J. I'm going home to my shitty trailer."

"Rob," Danny said. "Don't go. Come on. I'm sorry, man."

"I'm going to Brandon's place tomorrow to try and talk some sense into him. I might be poor, Danny, but at least I give a shit. If you figure out where you put your heart, give me a call and we can go together." I walked to the stairs, looked back. "Until then, go fuck yourself."

‖ PAUSE

Danny's words cut me to the bone. Only the best of friends can do that to each other. It's the fine line we walk between love and hate, and while those wounds will heal, they do leave scars. Some of them are quite deep.

A couple of years later, after we'd left Stauford for college—he with a full scholarship, me with a handful of government loans—I thanked him one night while we were drunk at a kegger. If he hadn't said what he'd said, I probably wouldn't have tried to prove him wrong. Poor or not, I made it my mission to get the hell out of that town, no matter what.

Would I have escaped Stauford otherwise?

Maybe, but these days I do wonder. What we walked into at Brandon Helmford's house would've sealed the deal for me, maybe for all of us. I'd be lying if I said the urge to hurt myself wasn't there, lingering in the back of my mind after that night, whispering to just do it, no one will care. I used to imagine that voice belonged to Hardy's ghost, lurking behind me like a shadow, trying to influence my actions.

Today I know better. That voice was always my own. We escaped Stauford, but we never escaped ourselves.

▶▶ FAST FWD

Saturday, October 24th, 1998. Hardy's Day, as I like to think of it.

Brandon Helmford lived in a rich neighborhood called Forest Hills. Normally, I would've avoided that place— the rich can always sniff out the poor, and my social status drew enough ridicule in school as it was—but that day I didn't care. Danny tried to call me twice that afternoon, and I let our answering machine pick up. The first time he hung up; the second time, he left a rambling apology and asked I call him back to "talk things over." I didn't. He'd already destroyed my pride in the span of five minutes, and I wanted to preserve the pieces that were left.

I tried reaching Nelle again, but she was offline. No email, either. I wish I'd called her. I don't know if it would've done any good, but goddammit, I wish I'd called anyway.

So, as the day went on, I psyched myself up for going solo to Brandon's. I don't know why it was such a big deal to me, going to his "party." Probably because I'd never been to a party before, and I'd certainly never crashed one. I was one of the social outcasts, a computer geek—inviting me to a party was a quick way to lose cred among your peers. Events like this always reminded me of how unprepared I was for college, or the world beyond.

Brandon's status was different. His image was by design, mostly just to piss off his conservative parents. He grew up with the social elite, still lived in their neighborhood, and his name still had weight. He had the freedom to be as weird or offensive as he wanted—he'd still be invited to all the parties because he was a Helmford.

So, when I parked down the street from his house, I wasn't surprised to see cars filling his driveway. Ain't no party like a Helmford party, and all that bullshit. I recognized some of the cars, including one that gave me pause. Nelle's metallic green VW bug. I'd know the paisley flower window stickers anywhere. Her presence worried me, but I shrugged it off. Of course she'd be at Brandon's party. I walked on.

One car I didn't expect to see was Danny's. He and Jordan climbed out and crossed the street to meet me.

"I wasn't sure if we'd missed you," Danny said. He stuck out his hand. "I'm sorry, Rob. I really am."

Reluctant, I shook his hand, but I didn't have an opportunity to say anything. A singular pop erupted from inside Brandon's house. Five more followed in succession. Dull flashes of light filled the windows on the first floor.

"Oh shit," Jordan whispered. "Were those—?"

"I think so," Danny said.

I didn't say anything. I ran up the sidewalk, the driveway, right to the front door. Didn't knock or ring the bell. The door was unlocked, so I barged in without thinking.

The first thing I remember is the stench of gunpowder. The air was full of it, a powerful odor that made my eyes water. There was something else, though—a mixture of incense, marijuana smoke, and metal. Especially metal, like iron or copper, so dense I tasted it on my tongue.

The slow strum of guitar blared from somewhere

else in the house. The foyer was empty, as was the adjacent stairway. I walked down the hall, following the slow musical hum, the pluck of guitar strings accompanied by a violin, and a singer's haunting voice. I recognized the band, and I remember smiling because they were Nelle's favorite: Mazzy Star. She must've selected the album to play. Of course she did. I can't imagine a better, more peaceful way to die.

I turned a corner into the living room.

I saw:

Hardy's face frozen on a massive television screen. Static interference and scanlines distorting the blood gushing from his nose, post-gunshot. His bloodshot eyes rolled up in his head.

Six kids—and they were kids to me, underclassmen, sophomores and juniors mostly—slack and crumpled into a massive sectional couch, blood gushing from their mouths and noses and the backs of their heads. Bits of bone and brain littered the back of the couch, and in my shock a ridiculous thought occurred to me: *They'll never get that stain out.* One of them was the kid I saw Brandon talking to yesterday. He was the last to go, his finger still curled around the trigger of a revolver.

An open box of ammunition lay on the coffee table before them like crayons, with six little soldiers missing. The VCR and TV remotes lay beside them.

Blood splatters on the wall. An impact crater from a bullet.

Cigarettes, joints, a couple of glasses of booze and a cheap bottle of vodka.

Gunsmoke snaking from the last kid's mouth, a

slow-moving tendril of dusty gray like his spirit waving one final goodbye.

Blood. God, there was so much blood. Dark, almost black, soaking into the carpet and drapery.

Their slack and wide-eyed expressions, frozen in permanent shock as if they'd been given the secret to the universe and it wasn't at all what they'd expected.

Their eyes, rolled up and staring into nothing, clouding with an absence of life.

The glow of television washing over the room, the erratic jitter of distortion painting them in a false light, animating their faces with film grain and static like the fallen harbinger before them.

Hardy's face taking shape over each of them like a death mask.

A stack of cassette cases on top of the television, just next to the VCR. All of them labeled with Video Fantastique's logo. How many times had they watched the video? How many times did the video repeat itself on a single cassette?

A single word came to mind, spelled out in slow and agonizing clarity just like the night before. O-T-H-E-R-S. Now I understood.

"Robby?" Danny's voice, just down the hall and a hundred miles away.

"Yeah," I said, my voice barely a whisper. I couldn't tear my eyes away from the grisly scene. *Don't come in here,* I wanted to say, but the words were lost from me. Something heavy hit the floor upstairs. Someone cried out—in terror or pain, I couldn't tell. And still I remained there, watching over the fallout of our curiosity, until Danny and Jordan snapped me from my trance.

"Oh my God." Jordan turned away and retched. Danny stood beside me, breathless, speechless. He opened his mouth and no words came.

From upstairs, more cries. Sobbing. Danny and I exchanged looks, a single name passing between our minds: *Nelle*.

We doubled back and raced upstairs, following the squeaking cries down a hallway toward a bedroom at the end. A poster of Marilyn Manson hung from a half-open door, and when I drew near, I smelled the sharp tang of incense. A black light glowed from a nightstand, illuminating a shivering shape on the bed. I flipped on the overhead light to get a better look.

Brandon Helmford huddled on his bed with a loop of speaker wire around his neck, sobbing so hard his body convulsed in stops and starts. Opposite the bed, the closet stood open, and when I saw Nelle's pale face, the world dropped away from me. What I'd witnessed downstairs should've prepared me for this, but I don't think any amount of desensitization could've helped me in that moment.

She'd hung herself with the same wire, one end tied around an exposed support beam above the closet. Her body hung forward at an angle, her neck bearing her body weight until she had no life left to give. Death wasn't instant, she had no way to snap her own neck, so gravity took care of her desires one agonizing second at a time. She looked almost peaceful, the way her head slumped to one side, and her dirty hair hid the wire digging into her throat.

"I tried to join her," Brandon stammered, "but the rack broke."

Bits of drywall and a pile of clothing lay on the

floor in the mouth of the closet beside Nelle. Brandon's weight pulled the clothes rack out of the wall, freeing him from the same fate, and I still wonder if he'd planned it that way, however unconscious a decision it might've been.

The rest happened in a blur. Danny and Jordan joined me upstairs at some point—it could've been seconds, but it felt like hours—and I had to leave the room while they cut her down because I couldn't recognize her face anymore. Hardy's face took shape over hers just like his victims downstairs. I say "victims" with intent. He influenced them into taking their lives. That desire to watch his death over and over, it was his way of urging us to join him. We were the others. Every one of us dies alone, but Hardy wanted company, and that day he got it.

I don't know who called the cops. It might've been Jordan, or it might've been a neighbor who'd heard the gunshots.

When I walked downstairs and saw the stack of VHS tapes on the TV, something inside me snapped. the feeling like the anxiety attack I'd had the day before. Racing heart, racing thoughts, rapid breathing, and buried at the center of it all was a single flame of anger burning away at me, pushing me forward, pushing me to *do something*, pushing me to *fix this*. I'd just lost a friend to this insanity, and I think I knew then that what had happened to her would happen to us unless I did something to stop it.

I didn't wait around for the cops. I didn't wait for Danny and Jordan to come downstairs. I left Brandon's house and drove to Breyersburg to confront Thomas Helmford.

▶ PLAY

There isn't much to say about it, really. I did it. I don't regret it.

The shop was still open when I got there, and I waited for a young couple to leave before going inside. They walked outside, empty-handed and confused. There was no one at the register, and no one answered when they rang the little bell on the desk. Thomas Helmford was already dead, had probably been dead for hours, and who knows how many customers arrived to rent a video only to leave with nothing.

I'd driven the fifteen miles in a seething rage, rehearsing in my mind the vitriol I would spew in Thomas's face. Instead, I found him at his computer, slumped backward in his chair, surrounded in a pool of his own blood and piss. His gun lay on the floor, a blood-stained offering to the god of television and entertainment. A pile of empty plastic cases lay to one side, each one sporting the Video Fantastique logo, while the clip of Hardy's suicide looped over and over on the screen in front of Helmford. A pack of cigarettes and a lighter sat near the desk's edge.

"You sick son of a bitch." I walked to the desk, lifted one of the cigarettes from the pack, and held the lighter in my hand. "I wish we'd never come here. I wish we'd never asked you about that stupid tape."

The TV on the desk flickered and froze. The other screens along the wall lit up and degaussed themselves, announcing the arrival of my old friend. Benjamin Hardy's bleeding face filled each screen, a dozen pale and grainy faces staring back at me with empty eyes.

O-T-H-E-R-S.

Joining him crossed my mind. The desire was still there, to join this bastard in the void, but I didn't waste time contemplating the choice. I lit the cigarette, took my first drag, and held the stinging smoke in my lungs for as long as I could before hacking it all up. That was the first cigarette of many, and I used it to commit an act of arson. When I'd collected myself, I took one of the VHS cassettes and unspooled the film. I held the cigarette's cherry ember to the edge and watched the flame spread.

I did this a few more times, starting multiple fires across the warehouse. I took another drag from the cigarette, steadied myself from the light-headedness of a nicotine rush, and wiped sweat from my brow. Benjamin Hardy's iterations all watched me without expression, the camera zooming in on his grainy face, each one distorting slightly. Changing. The eyes drooping, the nose elongating, the mouth twisting into a mess of blood and flesh.

Satisfied, I sucked down the last of the cigarette and tossed it into the bloody puddle at Helmford's feet.

Hardy's blank expression twisted into something like a smile, but I didn't stick around to be sure. Smoke filled the warehouse. The fire spread.

I drove a few miles down the highway and pulled over when I heard sirens. Two fire engines raced down the opposite side of the road. I sat there for a few minutes, listening to the radio, and screamed until I was hoarse. I screamed for Nelle. I screamed for Danny and Jordan.

But mostly, I screamed for me.

■ STOP

▷ PLAY

March 3rd, 2018

Long time since I wrote anything here.
Lots of things happened, but I'm too
tired to recap it all. All I'll say is I'm in
rehab. Met a friend. His name starts
with an H. Sort of like Hardy, but his
real name is Heron, and he's my best
friend. Better than the friends I had in
school.

But he's bad for me, too. Just like
Hardy was. Is. Because Hardy's still here.
I thought he was gone for a while, you
know? I was clean, sobering up, and then

one day I saw him downtown while I was driving through. Nearly crashed my car. And then I saw him again a few days later, on someone's face. The lady at the drugstore. A guy at the grocery store. My landlord. My boss.

You know how it goes. One thing leads to another, one fix leads to another, and when you're desperate enough to escape your demons you'll try anything. Anything. And I did, too. I tried anything I could, and that's how I met my friend Heroin. Jordan found Jesus and I found Heroin and Robby . . . well, he found art, I guess. I think about him sometimes. I wish I hadn't alienated him so much. Feel pretty shitty about that.

This rehab thing, I'm supposed to follow all these steps. One of them is keeping a journal, something I've tried to do over the years. One of them is making amends with all the folks I've wronged. Robby's at the top of that list, but I'll be damned if I can bring myself to call him or write. I'm afraid to.

I'm afraid that if I do, the dead man will find him. I'm scared that he'll find J. I'm scared that he won't give up until he has us all.

I'm scared, but I'll hold onto him as long as I can. For you, J. For you, Robby.

But I'm so scared, and this weight is so heavy.

▶▶ FAST FWD

THIS WAS DANNY'S last entry before his suicide note. Best I can figure, he thought he was keeping Hardy's ghost at bay somehow. And maybe he was, for a time. There were long stretches where I didn't see the dead man. Danny, if that was your doing, I thank you.

Me and Danny and Jordan didn't talk all that much after that night. We were so drained and devastated by Nelle's suicide that I think we just needed a break from each other. All three of us attended Nelle's funeral, but we didn't speak. There wasn't much left to say.

Brandon Helmford spent a week in the psych wing of Baptist Regional, and then a few months in extensive therapy. Last time I saw him, he was standing in the parking lot next to his van, smoking a cigarette. He'd lost weight, was little more than skin and bone, piercings and black nail polish. We locked eyes briefly, but neither of us spoke, and that was just as well. I didn't have anything good to say to him. A week later, Brandon's mom found him dead in the shower. He'd slit his wrists and bled out.

The break between my friends and I lasted until graduation, when we reconciled in celebration. College came, and while we tried to maintain that friendship, adulthood picked us apart and sent us along our separate paths. I lost touch with Danny and Jordan. I moved away, found a way to make a living with my writing. The ghost of Benjamin Hardy was never far away, though. He was still in my dreams, when I found myself standing in that room at the lectern, watching me from behind the old camera.

I picked up a nasty habit the night of the suicides. Two packs of smokes a day take a nasty toll on you, but when you've got anxiety like I do, you'll do anything to take the edge off. Nicotine helped until it didn't. Got my diagnosis just last week. Lung cancer. The doctor wants me to try chemo and other shit, anything to try and prolong my life and keep it from spreading, but I'm not keen on it. I'd rather go out on my own terms.

My own terms. That sounds so funny, because even now I'm trying to lie to myself.

Hardy watched me put that cigarette in my mouth. He smiled when I took one last drag. He knew he'd see me again, one way or another. Suicide is suicide, whether it happens in an instant or over a long stretch of time. Either way, he knew I was killing myself, and deep down, I think part of me knew it too. We all did.

Jordan suffered from depression, and he tried to treat it with religion, but not even Jesus could catch him when he jumped off that cliff. Danny found his vice in drugs, and I'd like to think he spent his final moments in a blissful stupor before the darkness claimed him.

Was it a curse for watching Hardy die? Did he silently curse anyone who watched his suicide, however unwitting a viewer they might have been?

He's still outside my window, and he's on my TV screen. He's on my computer as well. He's watched me all through tonight as I've written this confession. A silent editor, judging me for all my mistakes, watching from afar as I pace the floors and struggle against the pain inside my chest. Watching from my bedroom window as I pulled the safe from my closet and keyed in the combination. A .357 Magnum is heavier than you think. I bought it years ago, and I felt so silly at the time, but now I understand.

Is it that Hardy didn't want to be alone in death? Is that why he wanted O-T-H-E-R-S?

A man could go mad trying to answer those questions himself. A man could go mad from being stalked his whole life by a dead man, but sometimes, there's a stark sense of sanity in desperation.

SCANLINES

What does Congressman Hardy want from me?
What did he want from any of us?

I don't know, but after I finish this cigarette, I'm going to ask him.

■ S T O P

TELLING A FUCKING

just to figure out some of what makes me tick. You know? That my

AFTERWORD

If you've read this far, you're probably wondering how much of this story is true. Every writer will tell you there's a little truth in their fiction. And if they don't, they're either lying to you or to themselves. I won't lie to you—there's truth in these pages, and most of it is the uncomfortable variety.

Thing is, it didn't start this way. I had better intentions. The darkness came later.

The idea for this story accumulated from a few sources while I was on medical leave from my day job. I'd been struggling with a severe bout of anxiety and depression over many months. Taking a leave made the most sense, as did therapy, and I had to learn new ways of identifying and coping with my afflictions. Writing has always been my therapy. I think it's why my work tends to be so dark. I exorcise the demons on paper so they don't manifest elsewhere.

Anyway. I wanted to write something a bit lighter in tone. I'd just finished revising my novel, *Devil's Creek,* which is an extremely dark and heavy story. I needed a change. A coming-of-age story seemed like a good idea. I could write about my old friends, laugh at the stupidity of my adolescence, and dig into my past to figure out some of what makes me tick. You know. *Therapy*.

Right. Stupidity in my adolescence. There was that time my friends and I accidentally downloaded a video of Budd Dwyer's televised suicide. That was pretty stupid. Mr. Dwyer's blank expression post-gunshot is something I've never forgotten, so maybe I could explore the unspoken ramifications of witnessing such a horrific tragedy.

This was southeastern Kentucky in the '90s. Depression wasn't an illness, just something you went through from time to time, and you didn't talk about it. Going to see a shrink was an embarrassment because it meant you were "crazy" or "unhinged." You kept everything inside because boys don't cry and all that toxic bullshit.

So, I had the scenario for a story. Three teen friends deal with the effects of watching a traumatizing video of someone's suicide. That wasn't exactly the lighter coming-of-age tone I was going for, but I saw a potential for healing in the premise. There was something in my memories of the era, my friends, and my lifelong dealings with depression and anxiety that needed to be explored. Even if the story never saw the light of day, I could at least get these things out of my head for a while, and maybe figure something out about myself in the process.

There were other truths, though. The income disparity, for one. Me spending a lot of time at my friend's house because I needed to get away from my parents. Being alone at home because my parents were always working. My crush on Nelle's real-world counterpart. The great music. The dangerous, mysterious, untamed nature of the internet. So much angst and misplaced anger.

And then there was the recursive nature of trauma. How it always seems to feed into itself and resurface over and over again.

Yeah, I had a lot to work through, and by the end the story wasn't at all what I imagined it would be. It had grown into something I didn't recognize at first. A dark story of curiosity and tragedy and suicide. A ghost story, but not the conventional sort. Benjamin Hardy is less a ghost than he is the force of depression. He's the grim face you see projected on everyone else, that same face you see in the mirror every day, the one that tells you there's no point, you aren't worth it, you don't deserve it, and why not end it already? He's the liar in your head, and you're the suit he wears.

By the end, I realized I'd done what I'd set out to do. I'd participated in an act of therapy, and the result is something that still scares the shit out of me. How easily one can slip from depression to suicide if they aren't careful. How easily that emptiness inside can consume you if you listen to its lies.

I'm proud of *Scanlines*, but I'm not proud of where it came from. I had to shine a light on some shadows inside myself, and I don't think I was ready to look at them just yet. But then again, are we ever?

Todd Keisling
Womelsdorf, Pennsylvania
December 21st, 2020

ACKNOWLEDGEMENTS

We never write these things alone, do we? There's always someone waiting on the sidelines, or perhaps at the end of the tunnel, usually cheering us on. Sometimes they even have a flashlight to guide us home. The following folks showed me the way:

Thank you, Sam Cowan, for giving this book life at Dim Shores. Thank you, Max and Lori, for resurrecting it with Perpetual Motion Machine Publishing. And thank you, Matt Revert, for the deliciously grim cover design.

Love and gratitude to my wife, Erica, for encouraging me to pursue this story despite its dark nature. She's the light that guides me home every time.

Many thanks to my friends and beta readers, Amelia Bennett, Brian Kirk, Nikki Nelson-Hicks, Anthony J. Rapino, David Rockey, R.B. Wood, and Mercedes M. Yardley for the advice, feedback, and support.

Finally, for the real Danny and Jordan: Thanks for letting me kill you on the page. I promise it's a symbol of endearment.

ABOUT THE AUTHOR

TODD KEISLING is the Bram Stoker Award-nominated author of *Devil's Creek*. His other books include *The Final Reconciliation*, *Ugly Little Things: Collected Horrors*, and *The Monochrome Trilogy*, among several shorter works. He lives somewhere in the wilds of Pennsylvania with his family where he is at work on his next novel.

IF YOU ENJOYED
SCANLINES, DON'T MISS
THESE OTHER TITLES FROM
PERPETUAL MOTION
MACHINE . . .

LOST SIGNALS
EDITED BY MAX BOOTH III AND
LORI MICHELLE

ISBN: 978-1-943720-08-8

$16.95

What's that sound? Do you feel it?

The signals are already inside you. You never even had a chance.

A tome of horror fiction featuring radio waves, numbers stations, rogue transmissions, and other unimaginable sounds you only wish were fiction. Forget about what's hiding in the shadows, and start worrying about what's hiding in the dead air.

With stories by Matthew M. Bartlett, T.E. Grau, Joseph Bouthiette Jr., Josh Malerman, David James Keaton, Tony Burgess, Michael Paul Gonzalez, George Cotronis, Betty Rocksteady, Christopher Slatsky, Amanda Hard, Gabino Iglesias, Dyer Wilk, Ashlee Scheuerman, Matt Andrew, H.F. Arnold, John C. Foster, Vince Darcangelo, Regina Solomond, Joshua Chaplinsky, Damien Angelica Walters, Paul Michael Anderson, and James Newman. Also includes an introduction from World Fantasy-award-winning author, Scott Nicolay.

LOST FILMS
EDITED BY MAX BOOTH III
AND LORI MICHELLE

ISBN: 978-1-943720-29-3
$18.95

From the editors of Lost Signals comes the new volume in technological horror. Nineteen authors, both respected and new to the genre, team up to deliver a collection of terrifying, eclectic stories guaranteed to unsettle its readers. In Lost Films, a deranged group of lunatics hold an annual film festival, the lost series finale of The Simpsons corrupts a young boy's sanity, and a VCR threatens to destroy reality. All of that and much more, with fiction from Brian Evenson, Gemma Files, Kelby Losack, Bob Pastorella, Brian Asman, Leigh Harlen, Dustin Katz, Andrew Novak, Betty Rocksteady, John C. Foster, Ashlee Scheuerman, Eugenia M. Triantafyllou, Kev Harrison, Thomas Joyce, Jessica McHugh, Kristi DeMeester, Izzy Lee, Chad Stroup, and David James Keaton.

THE GIRL IN THE VIDEO
BY MICHAEL DAVID WILSON
ISBN: 978-1-943720-43-9

$12.95

TELL ME WHAT YOU LIKE.

After a teacher receives a weirdly arousing video, his life descends into paranoia and obsession. More videos follow—each containing information no stranger could possibly know. But who's sending them? And what do they want? The answers may destroy everything and everyone he loves.

The Perpetual Motion Machine Catalog

PERPETUAL MOTION MACHINE PUBLISHING

Patreon:
www.patreon.com/pmmpublishing

Website:
www.PerpetualPublishing.com

Facebook:
www.facebook.com/PerpetualPublishing

Twitter:
@PMMPublishing

Newsletter:
www.PMMPNews.com

Email Us:
Contact@PerpetualPublishing.com

9 781943 720583